THE HARDY BOYS

Undercover Brothers®

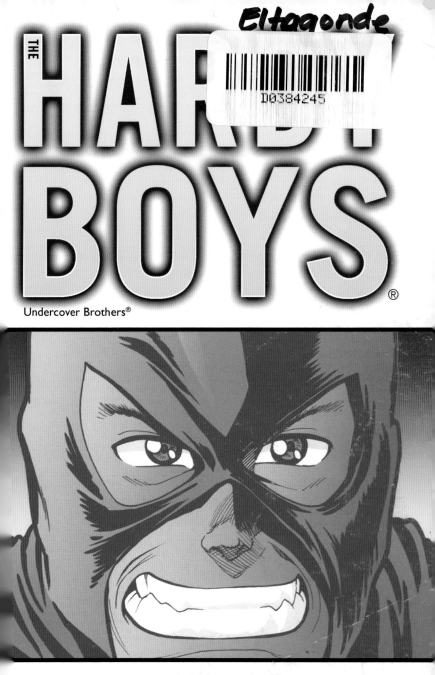

PAPERCUTZ™

THE HARDY BOYS GRAPHIC NOVELS FROM PAPERCUTZ

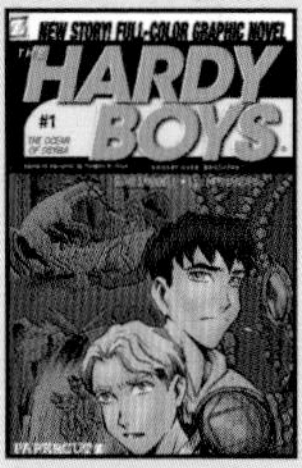
NEW STORY! FULL-COLOR GRAPHIC NOVEL
HARDY BOYS
#1
PAPERCUTZ
#1"The Ocean of Osyria"

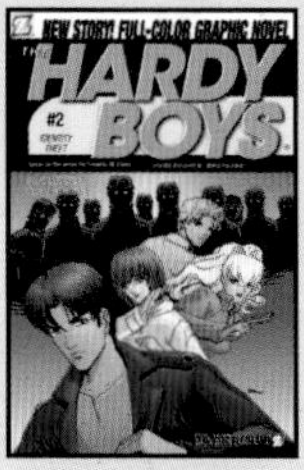
NEW STORY! FULL-COLOR GRAPHIC NOVEL
HARDY BOYS
#2
PAPERCUTZ
#2 "Identity Theft"

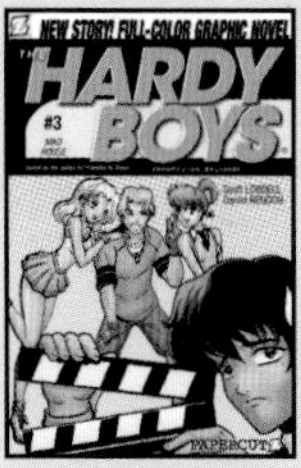
NEW STORY! FULL-COLOR GRAPHIC NOVEL
HARDY BOYS
#3
PAPERCUTZ
#3 "Mad House"

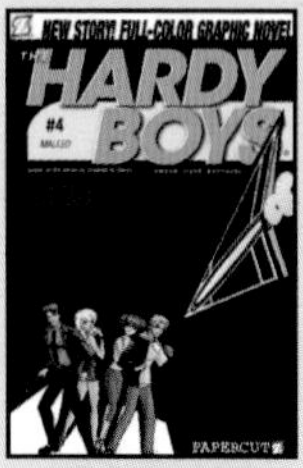
NEW STORY! FULL-COLOR GRAPHIC NOVEL
HARDY BOYS
#4
PAPERCUTZ
#4 "Malled"

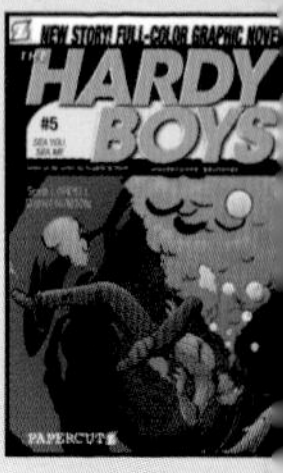
HARDY BOYS
#5
PAPERCUTZ
#5 "Sea You, Sea Me!"

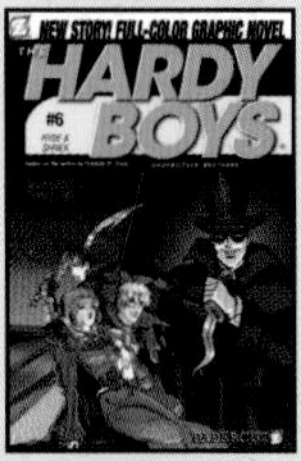
NEW STORY! FULL-COLOR GRAPHIC NOVEL
HARDY BOYS
#6
PAPERCUTZ
#6 "Hyde & Shriek"

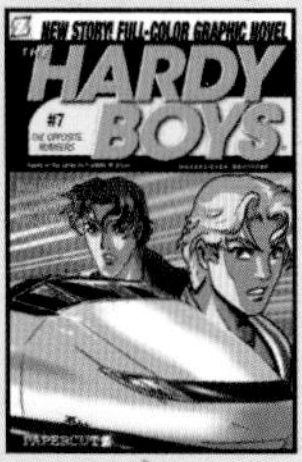
NEW STORY! FULL-COLOR GRAPHIC NOVEL
HARDY BOYS
#7
PAPERCUTZ
#7 "The Opposite Numbers"

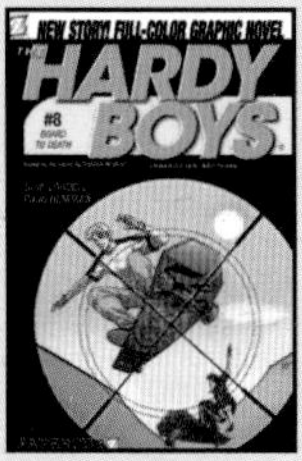
NEW STORY! FULL-COLOR GRAPHIC NOVEL
HARDY BOYS
#8
PAPERCUTZ
#8 "Board To Death"

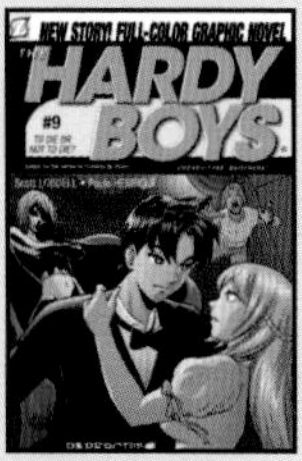
NEW STORY! FULL-COLOR GRAPHIC NOVEL
HARDY BOYS
#9
PAPERCUTZ
#9 "To Die Or Not To Die?"

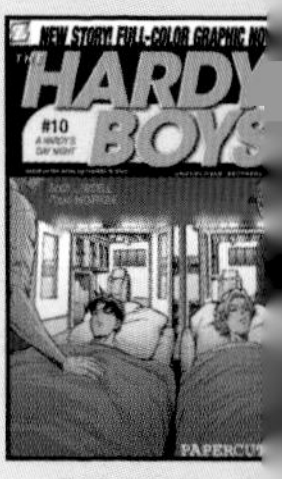
HARDY BOYS
#10
#10 "A Hard Day's Night"

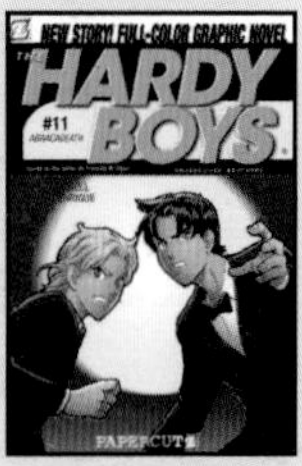
NEW STORY! FULL-COLOR GRAPHIC NOVEL
HARDY BOYS
#11
PAPERCUTZ
#11 "Abracadeath"

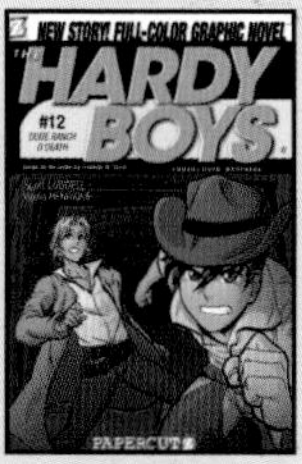
NEW STORY! FULL-COLOR GRAPHIC NOVEL
HARDY BOYS
#12
PAPERCUTZ
#12 "Dude Ranch O' Death!"

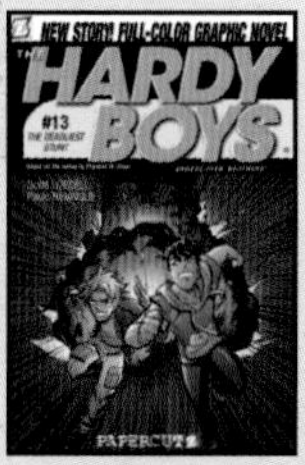
NEW STORY! FULL-COLOR GRAPHIC NOVEL
HARDY BOYS
#13
PAPERCUTZ
#13 "The Deadliest Stunt"

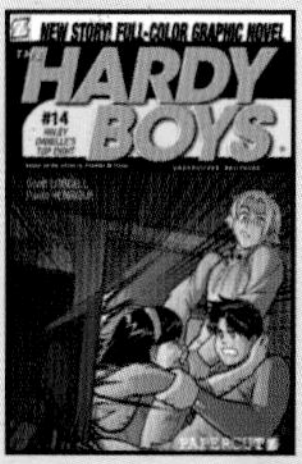
NEW STORY! FULL-COLOR GRAPHIC NOVEL
HARDY BOYS
#14
PAPERCUTZ
#14 "Haley Danelle's Top Eight!"

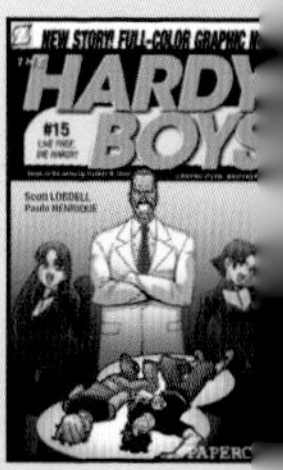
HARDY BOYS
#15
Scott LOBDELL
Paulo HENRIQUE
#15 "Live Fre Die Hardy!"

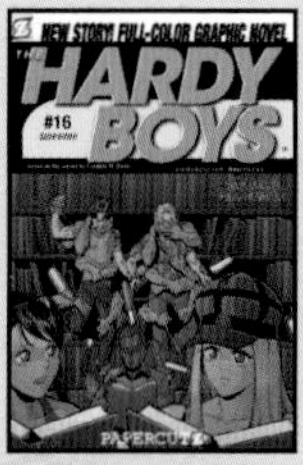
NEW STORY! FULL-COLOR GRAPHIC NOVEL
HARDY BOYS
#16
PAPERCUTZ
#16 "Shhhhhh!"

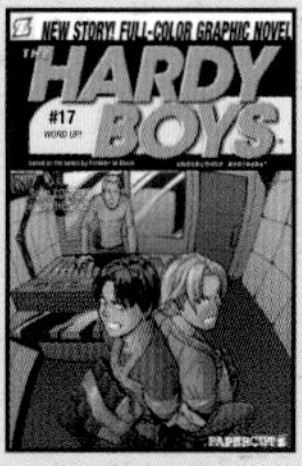
NEW STORY! FULL-COLOR GRAPHIC NOVEL
HARDY BOYS
#17
PAPERCUTZ
#17 "Word Up!"

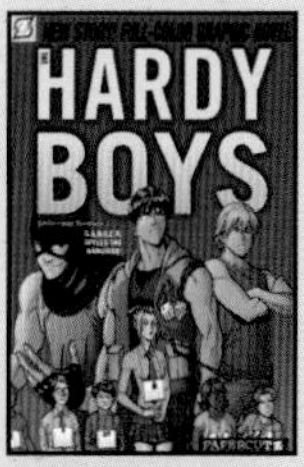
HARDY BOYS
PAPERCUTZ
#18 "D.A.N.G.E.R. Spells the Hangman"

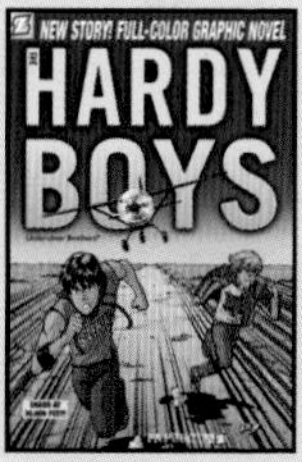
NEW STORY! FULL-COLOR GRAPHIC NOVEL
HARDY BOYS
Coming Soon! #19 "Chaos at 30,000 Feet!"

$7.95 each in paperback, $12.95 each in hardcover.

Please add $4.00 for postage and handling for the first book, add $1.00 for each additional book. Please make check payable to NBM Publishing. Send to: **Papercutz, 40 Exchange Plac Suite 1308, New York, NY 10005 • 1-800-886-1223 • www.papercutz.com**

THE HARDY BOYS

Undercover Brothers®

#18
D.A.N.G.E.R. Spells the Hangman

SCOTT LOBDELL • Writer
PAULO HENRIQUE MARCONDES • Artist

Based on the series by
FRANKLIN W. DIXON

New York

D.A.N.G.E.R. Spells the Hangman
SCOTT LOBDELL — Writer
PAULO HENRIQUE MARCONDES — Artist
MARK LERER — Letterer
LAURIE E. SMITH — Colorist
CHRIS NELSON AND SHELLY DUTCHAK — Production
MICHAEL PETRANEK — Editorial Assistant
JIM SALICRUP
Editor-in-Chief

ISBN: 978-1-59707-160-4 paperback edition
ISBN: 978-1-59707-161-1 hardcover edition

Distributed by Macmillan

Printed in China June 2009
by New Era Printing Limited
Room 1101-1103, Trende Centre
29-31 Cheung Lee St
Chai Wan, Hong Kong

10 9 8 7 6 5 4 3 2 1

CHAPTER ONE: "PAINT THAT A SHAME!"

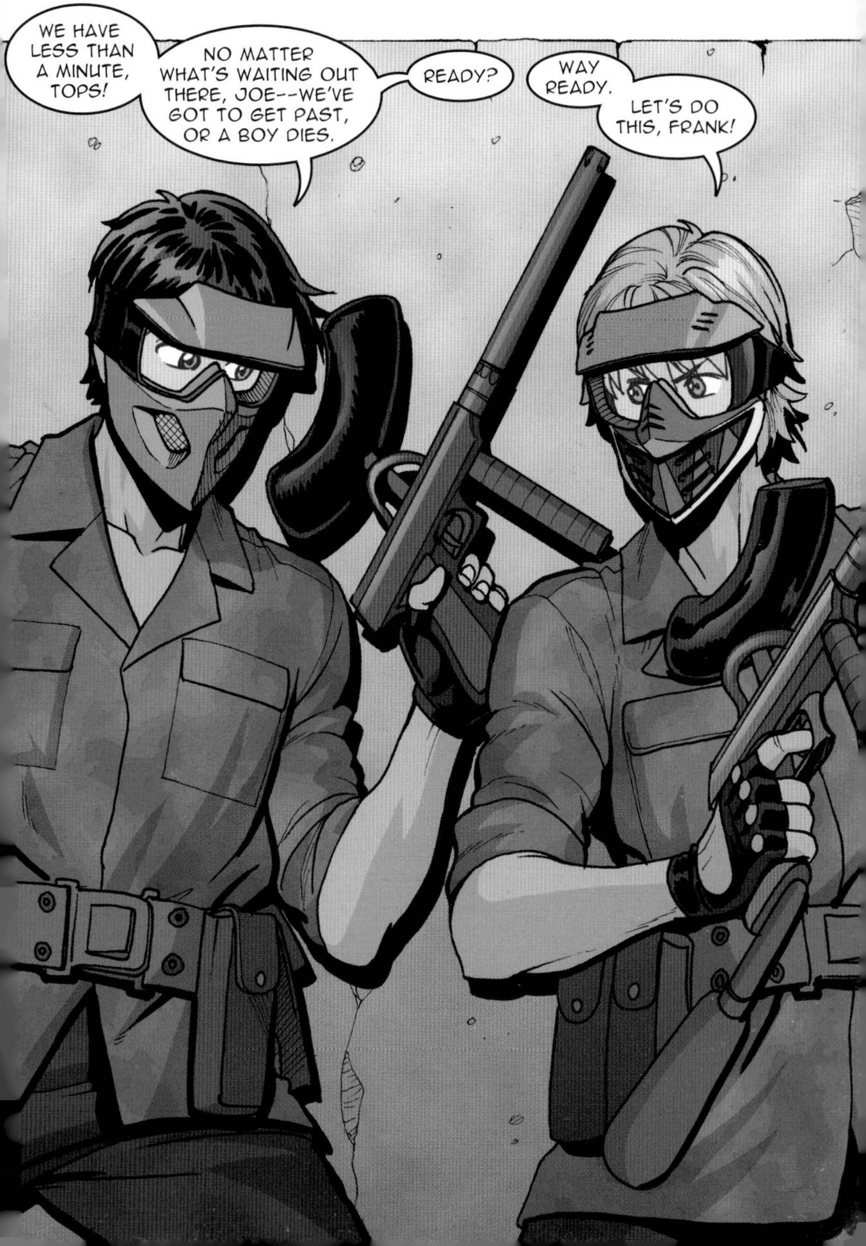
WE HAVE LESS THAN A MINUTE, TOPS!
NO MATTER WHAT'S WAITING OUT THERE, JOE--WE'VE GOT TO GET PAST, OR A BOY DIES.
READY?
WAY READY.
LET'S DO THIS, FRANK!

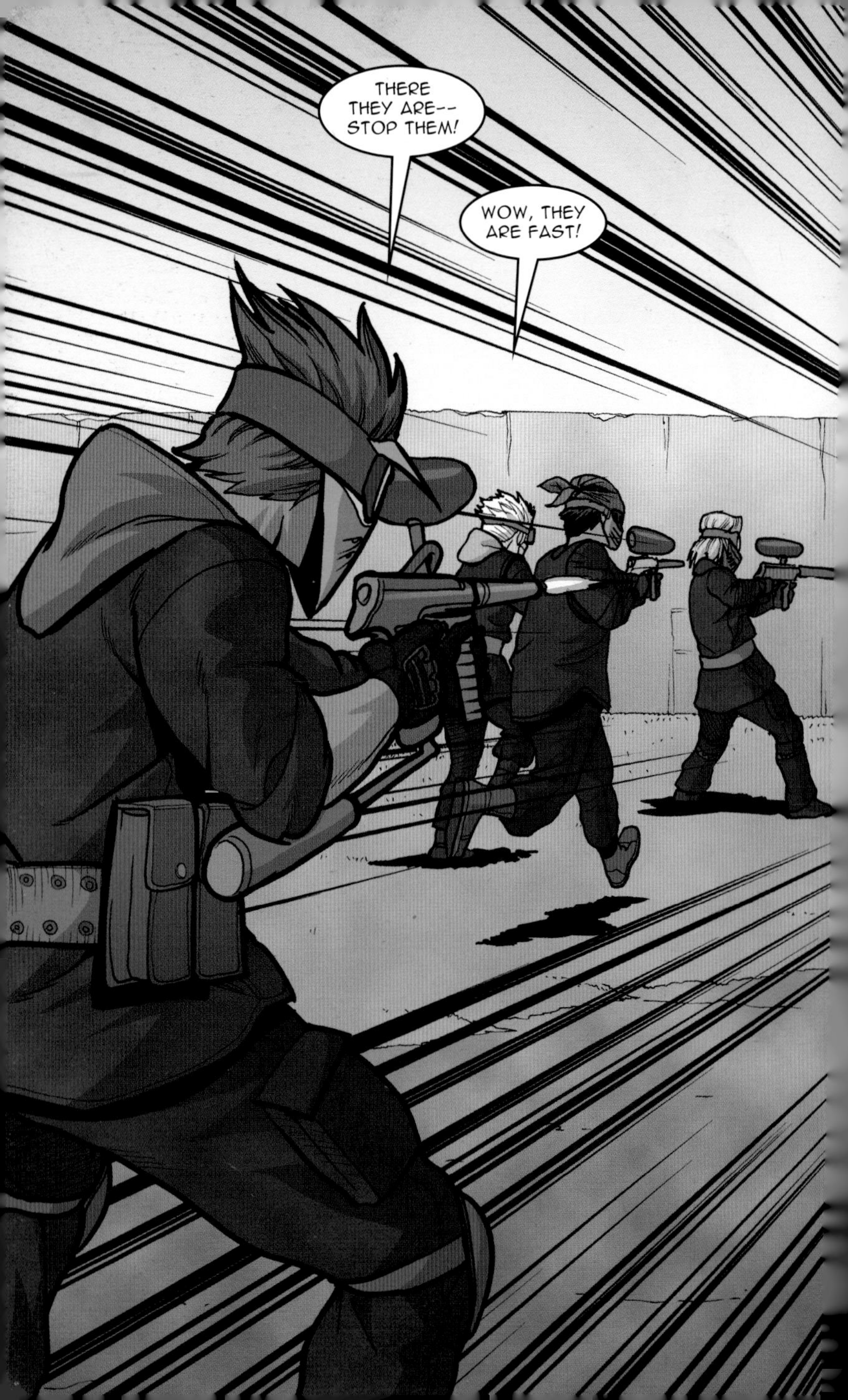
THERE THEY ARE-- STOP THEM!
WOW, THEY ARE FAST!

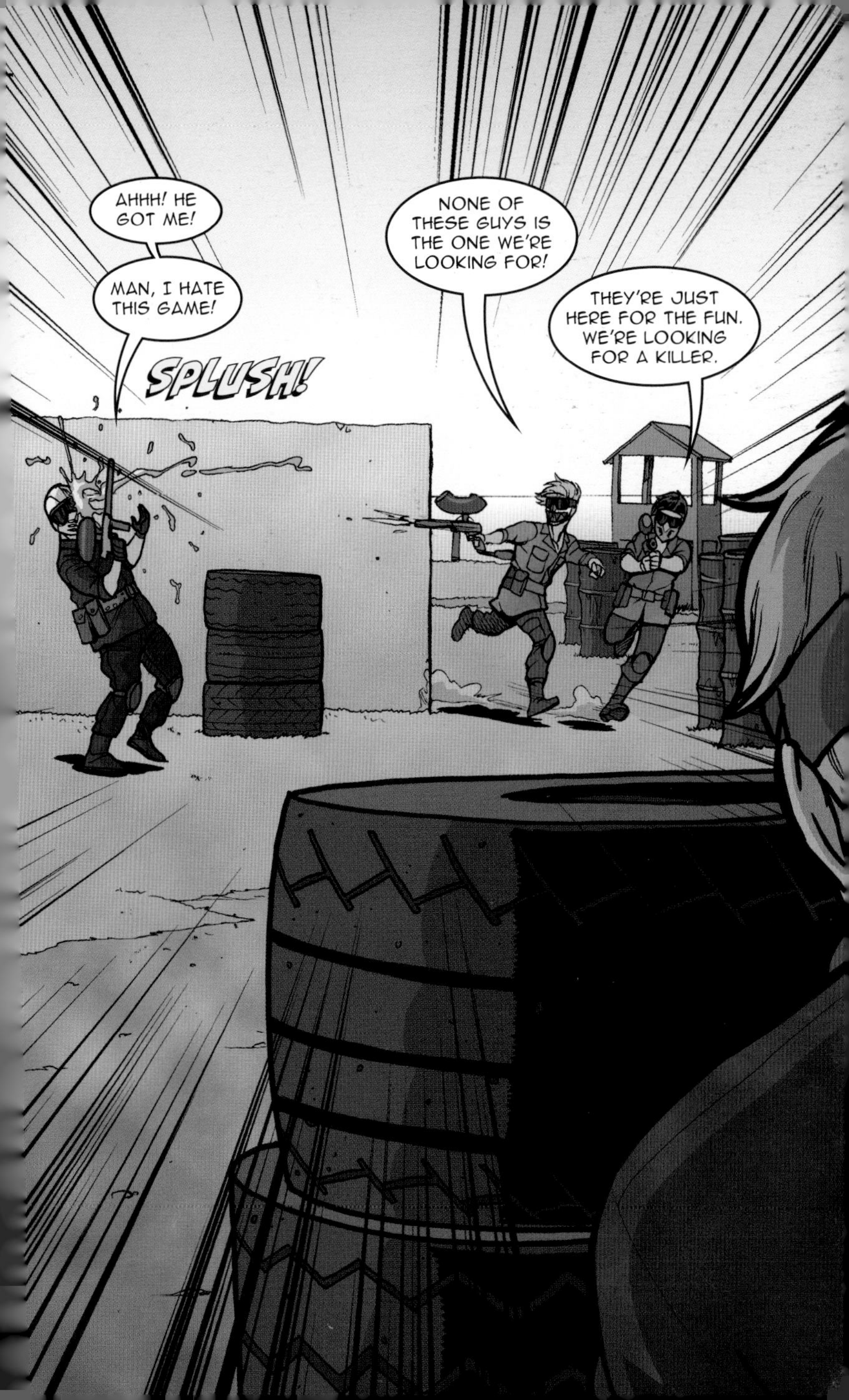
AHHH! HE GOT ME!
MAN, I HATE THIS GAME!
SPLUSH!
NONE OF THESE GUYS IS THE ONE WE'RE LOOKING FOR!
THEY'RE JUST HERE FOR THE FUN. WE'RE LOOKING FOR A KILLER.

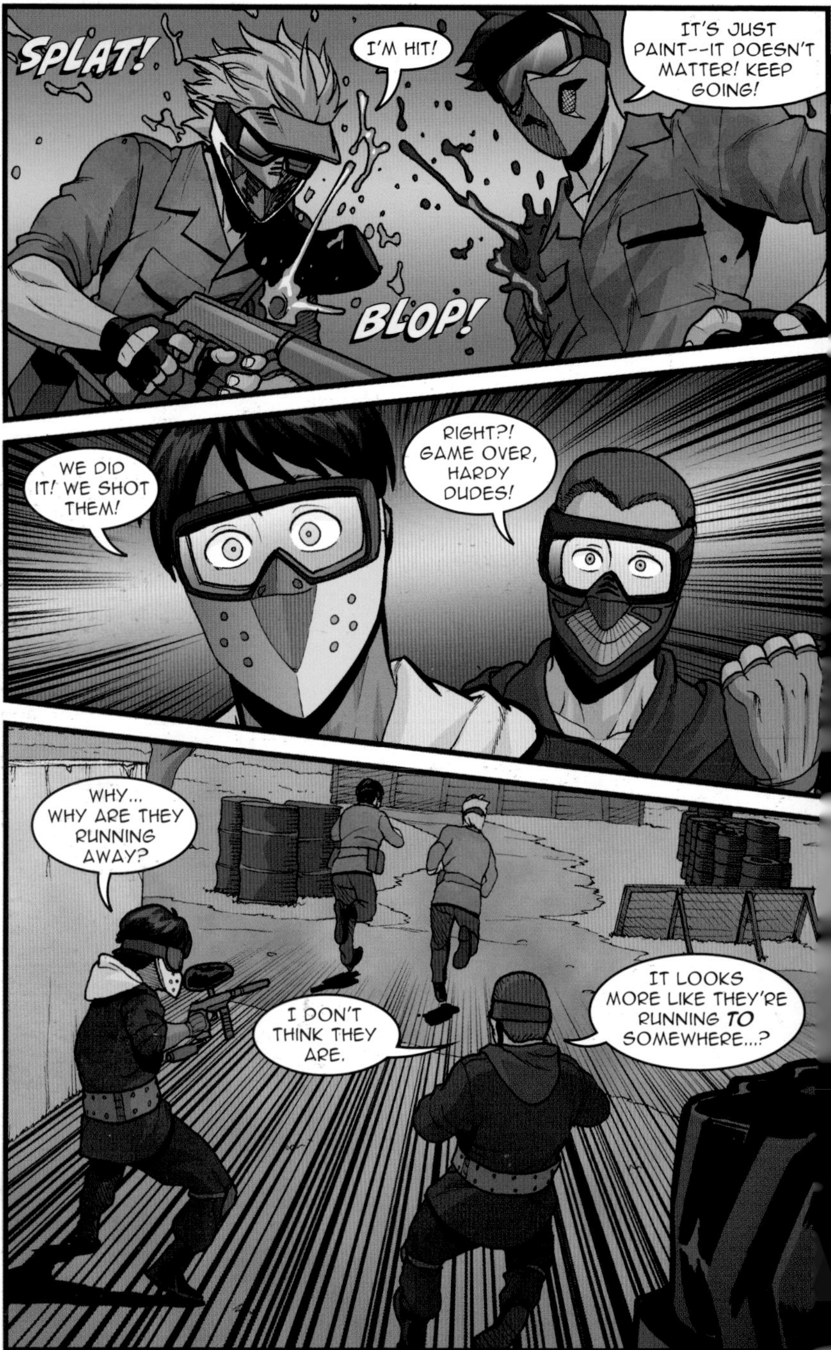
SPLAT!
I'M HIT!
IT'S JUST PAINT--IT DOESN'T MATTER! KEEP GOING!
BLOP!
WE DID IT! WE SHOT THEM!
RIGHT?! GAME OVER, HARDY DUDES!
WHY... WHY ARE THEY RUNNING AWAY?
I DON'T THINK THEY ARE.
IT LOOKS MORE LIKE THEY'RE RUNNING *TO* SOMEWHERE...?

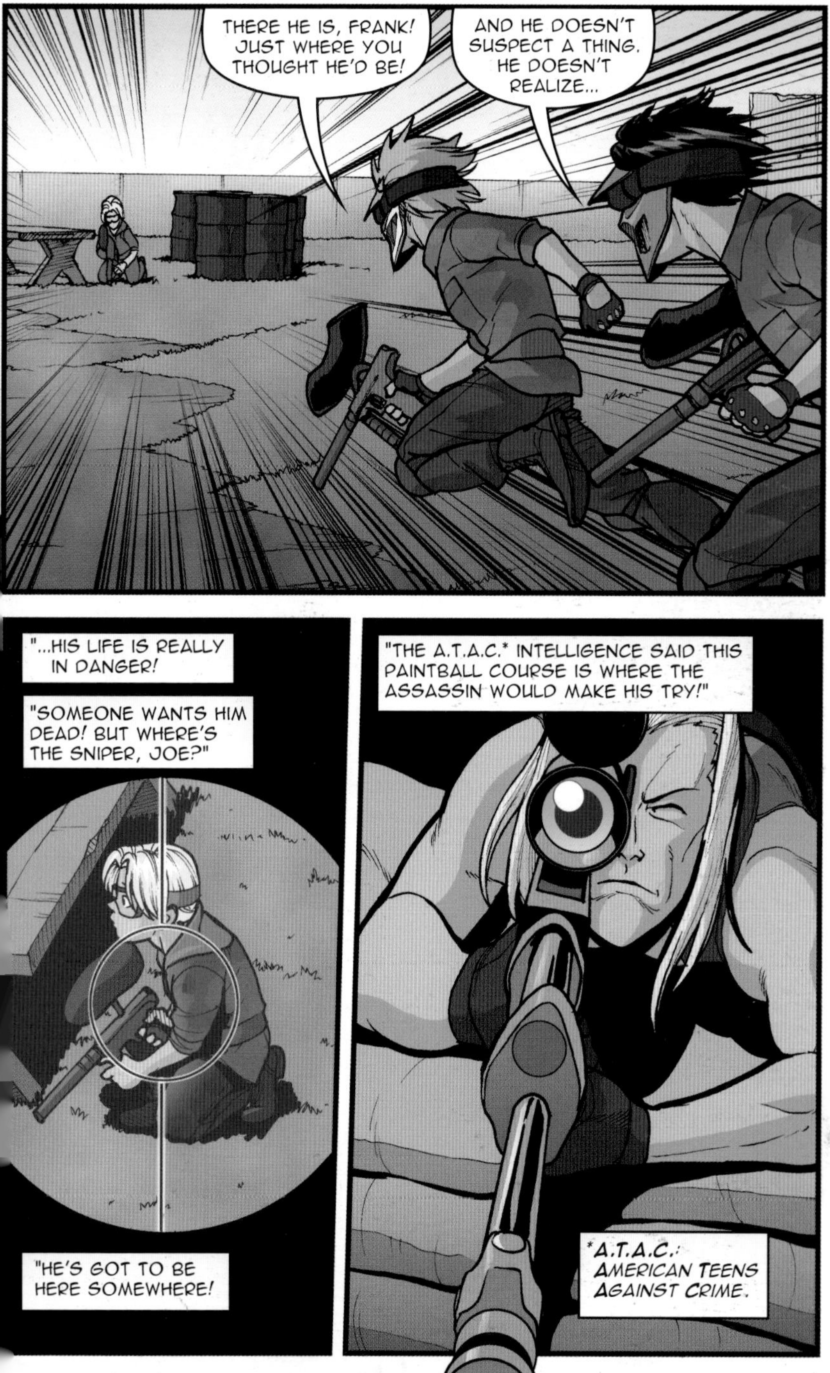
THERE HE IS, FRANK! JUST WHERE YOU THOUGHT HE'D BE!
AND HE DOESN'T SUSPECT A THING. HE DOESN'T REALIZE...
"...HIS LIFE IS REALLY IN DANGER!
"SOMEONE WANTS HIM DEAD! BUT WHERE'S THE SNIPER, JOE?"
"HE'S GOT TO BE HERE SOMEWHERE!
"THE A.T.A.C.* INTELLIGENCE SAID THIS PAINTBALL COURSE IS WHERE THE ASSASSIN WOULD MAKE HIS TRY!"
*A.T.A.C.: AMERICAN TEENS AGAINST CRIME.

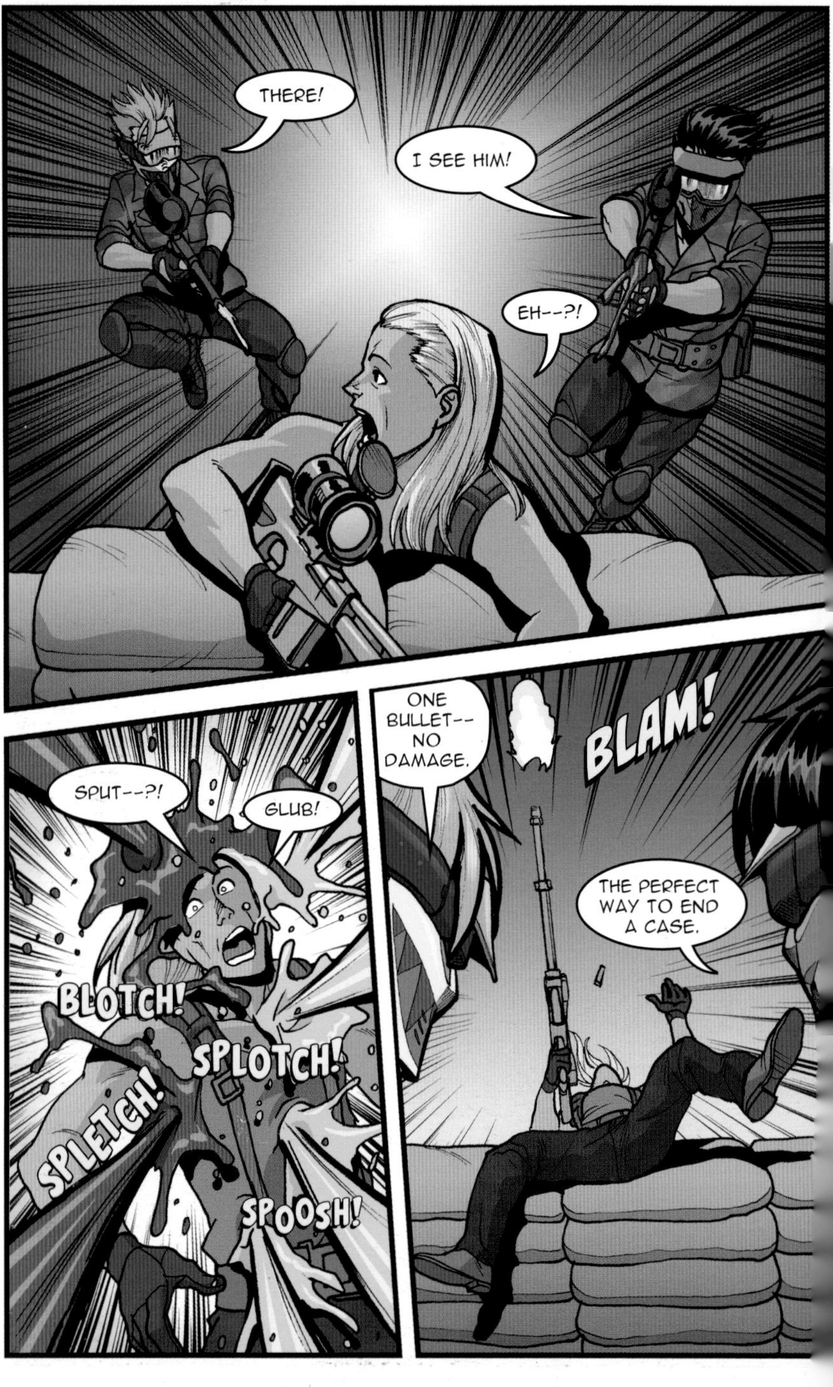
THERE!
I SEE HIM!
EH--?!
SPUT--?!
GLUB!
BLOTCH!
SPLOTCH!
SPLETCH!
SPOOSH!
ONE BULLET-- NO DAMAGE.
BLAM!
THE PERFECT WAY TO END A CASE.

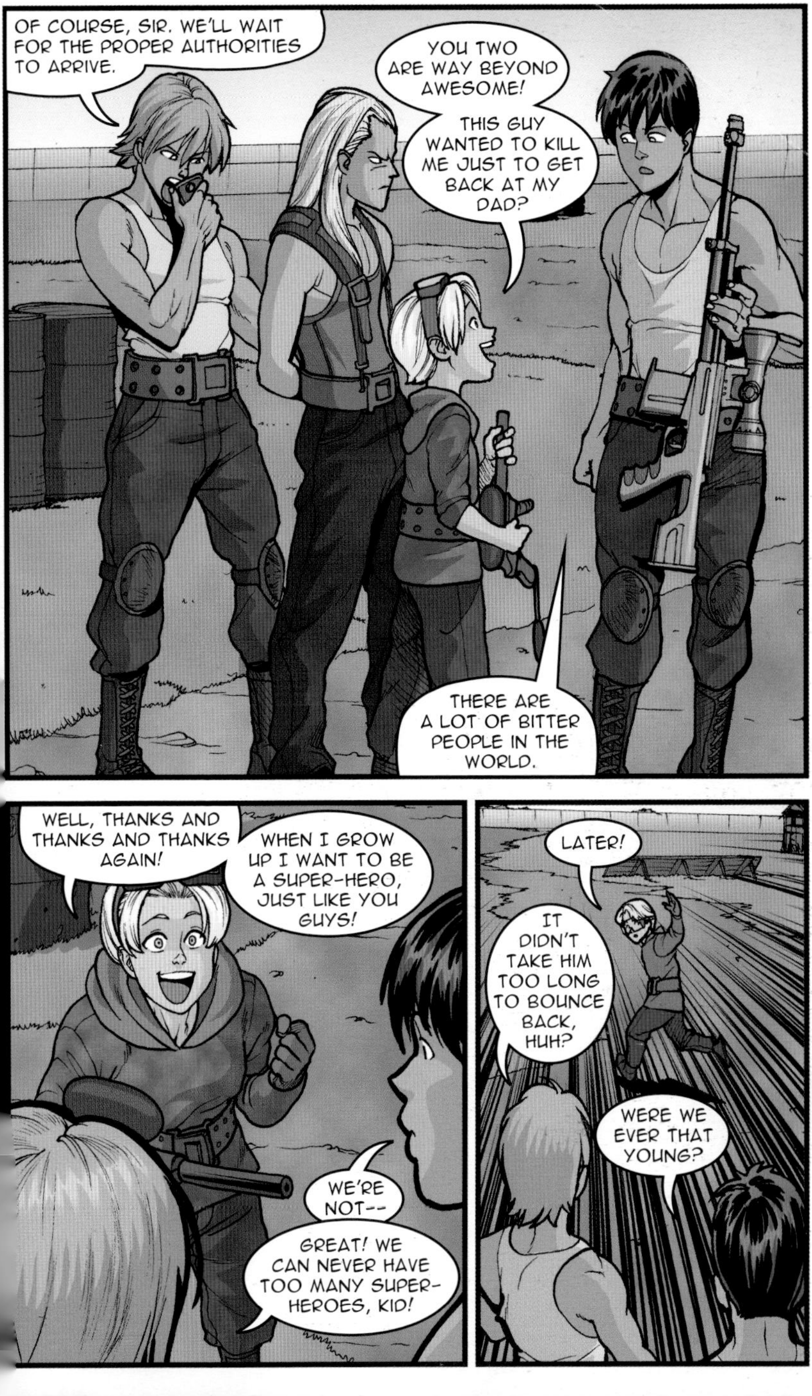

OF COURSE, SIR. WE'LL WAIT FOR THE PROPER AUTHORITIES TO ARRIVE.
YOU TWO ARE WAY BEYOND AWESOME!
THIS GUY WANTED TO KILL ME JUST TO GET BACK AT MY DAD?
THERE ARE A LOT OF BITTER PEOPLE IN THE WORLD.
WELL, THANKS AND THANKS AND THANKS AGAIN!
WHEN I GROW UP I WANT TO BE A SUPER-HERO, JUST LIKE YOU GUYS!
WE'RE NOT--
GREAT! WE CAN NEVER HAVE TOO MANY SUPER-HEROES, KID!
LATER!
IT DIDN'T TAKE HIM TOO LONG TO BOUNCE BACK, HUH?
WERE WE EVER THAT YOUNG?

CHAPTER TWO: "SPELLING BEE"
SEVERAL DAYS LATER, AT BAYPORT HIGH SCHOOL...
I'M SO PLEASED TO ANNOUNCE THAT OUR SCHOOL WILL BE REPRESENTED AT THE STATE SPELLING BEE, BY MISS CASSIE LONDON.
I'M HONORED, MRS. BARTLETT.
H. O. N. O. R. E. D.

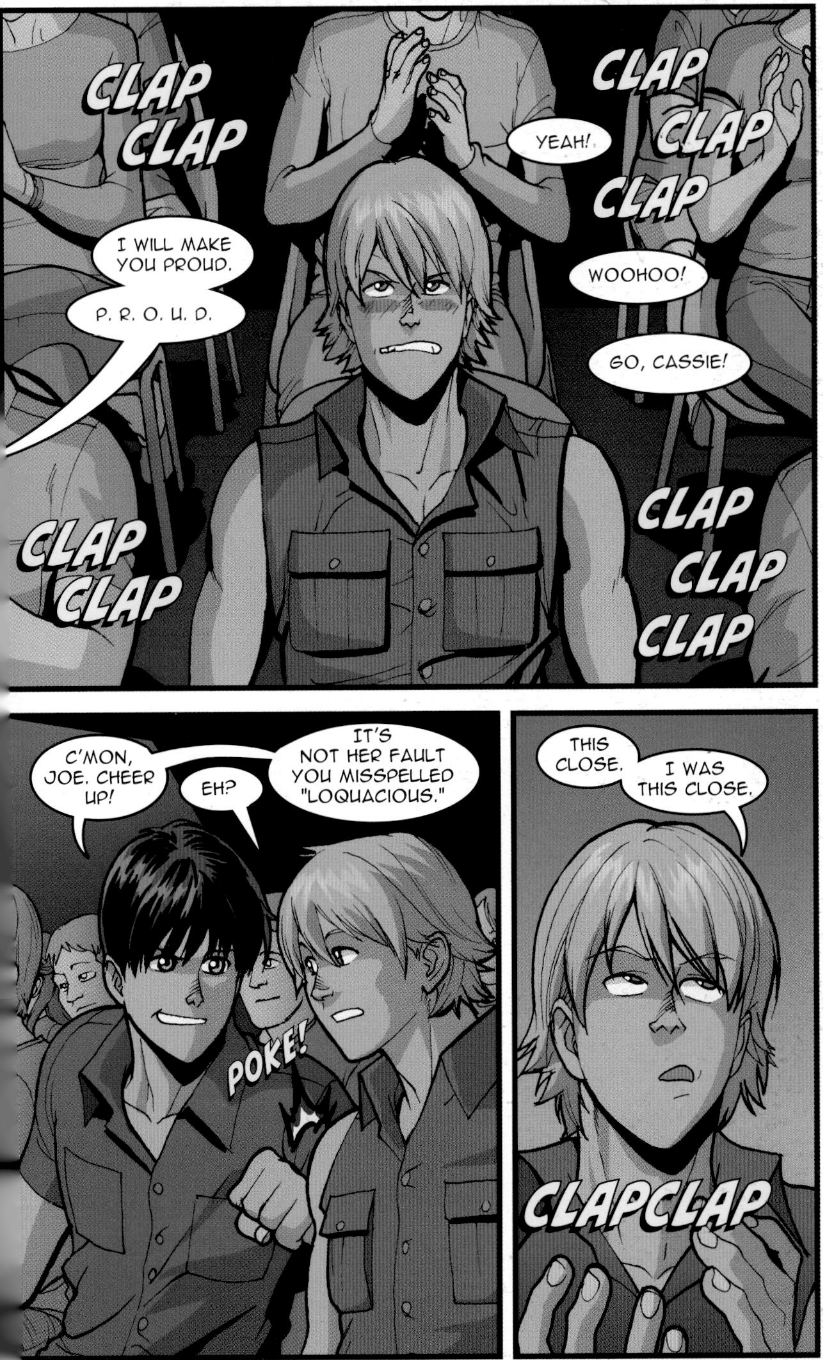
CLAP
CLAP
YEAH!
CLAP
CLAP
CLAP
I WILL MAKE YOU PROUD.
P. R. O. U. D.
WOOHOO!
GO, CASSIE!
CLAP
CLAP
CLAP
CLAP
CLAP
C'MON, JOE. CHEER UP!
EH?
IT'S NOT HER FAULT YOU MISSPELLED "LOQUACIOUS."
POKE!
THIS CLOSE.
I WAS THIS CLOSE.
CLAPCLAP

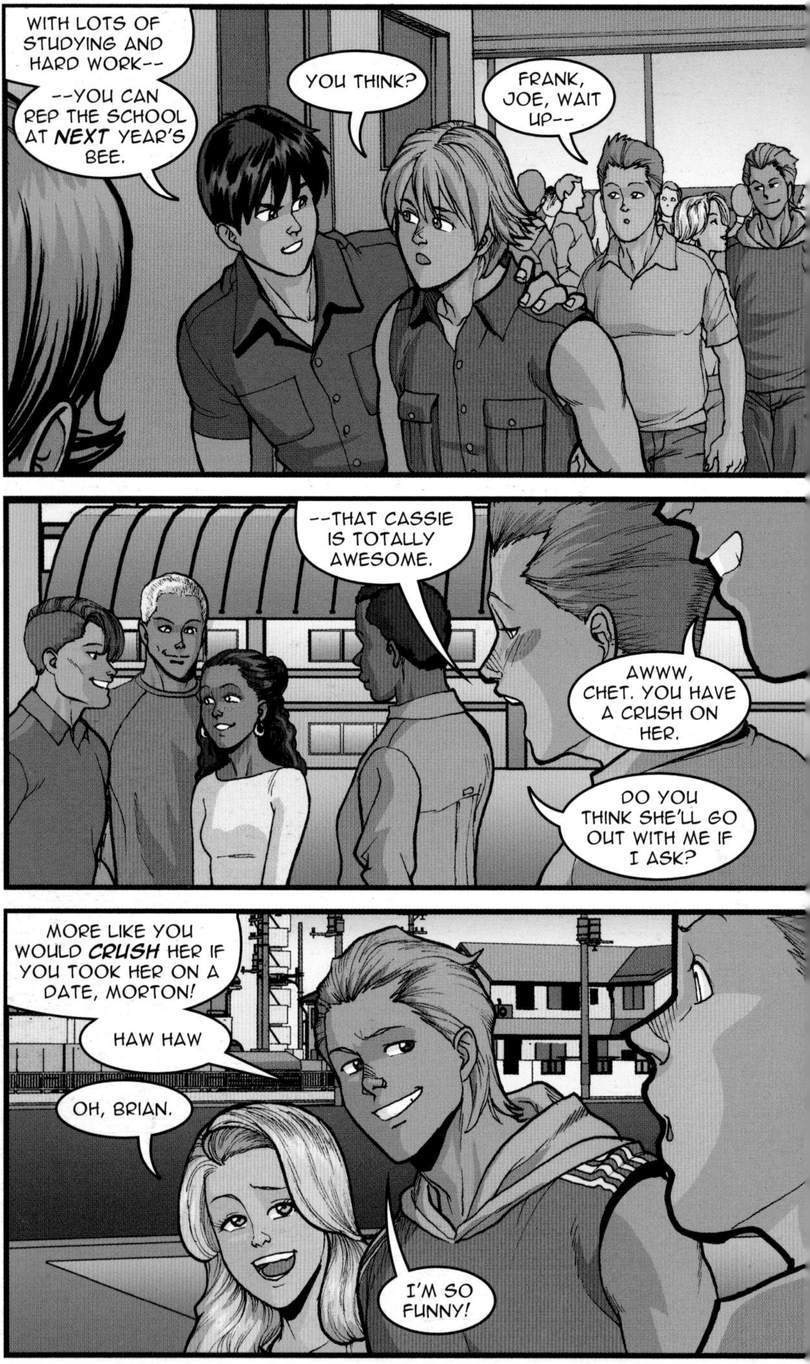
WITH LOTS OF STUDYING AND HARD WORK--
--YOU CAN REP THE SCHOOL AT **NEXT** YEAR'S BEE.
YOU THINK?
FRANK, JOE, WAIT UP--
--THAT CASSIE IS TOTALLY AWESOME.
AWWW, CHET. YOU HAVE A CRUSH ON HER.
DO YOU THINK SHE'LL GO OUT WITH ME IF I ASK?
MORE LIKE YOU WOULD **CRUSH** HER IF YOU TOOK HER ON A DATE, MORTON!
HAW HAW
OH, BRIAN.
I'M SO FUNNY!

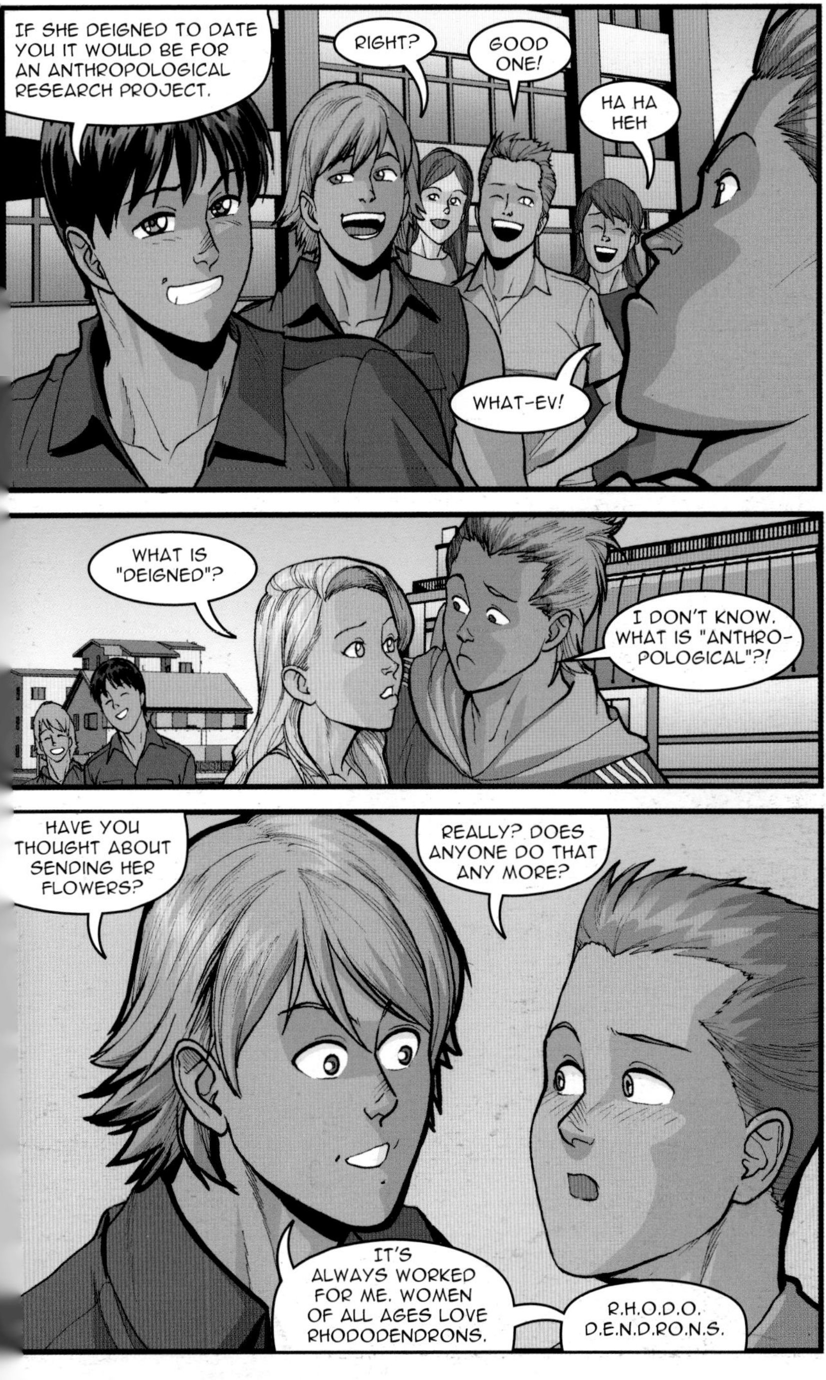
IF SHE DEIGNED TO DATE YOU IT WOULD BE FOR AN ANTHROPOLOGICAL RESEARCH PROJECT.
RIGHT?
GOOD ONE!
HA HA HEH
WHAT-EV!
WHAT IS "DEIGNED"?
I DON'T KNOW. WHAT IS "ANTHRO-POLOGICAL"?!
HAVE YOU THOUGHT ABOUT SENDING HER FLOWERS?
REALLY? DOES ANYONE DO THAT ANY MORE?
IT'S ALWAYS WORKED FOR ME. WOMEN OF ALL AGES LOVE RHODODENDRONS.
R.H.O.D.O. D.E.N.D.RO.N.S.

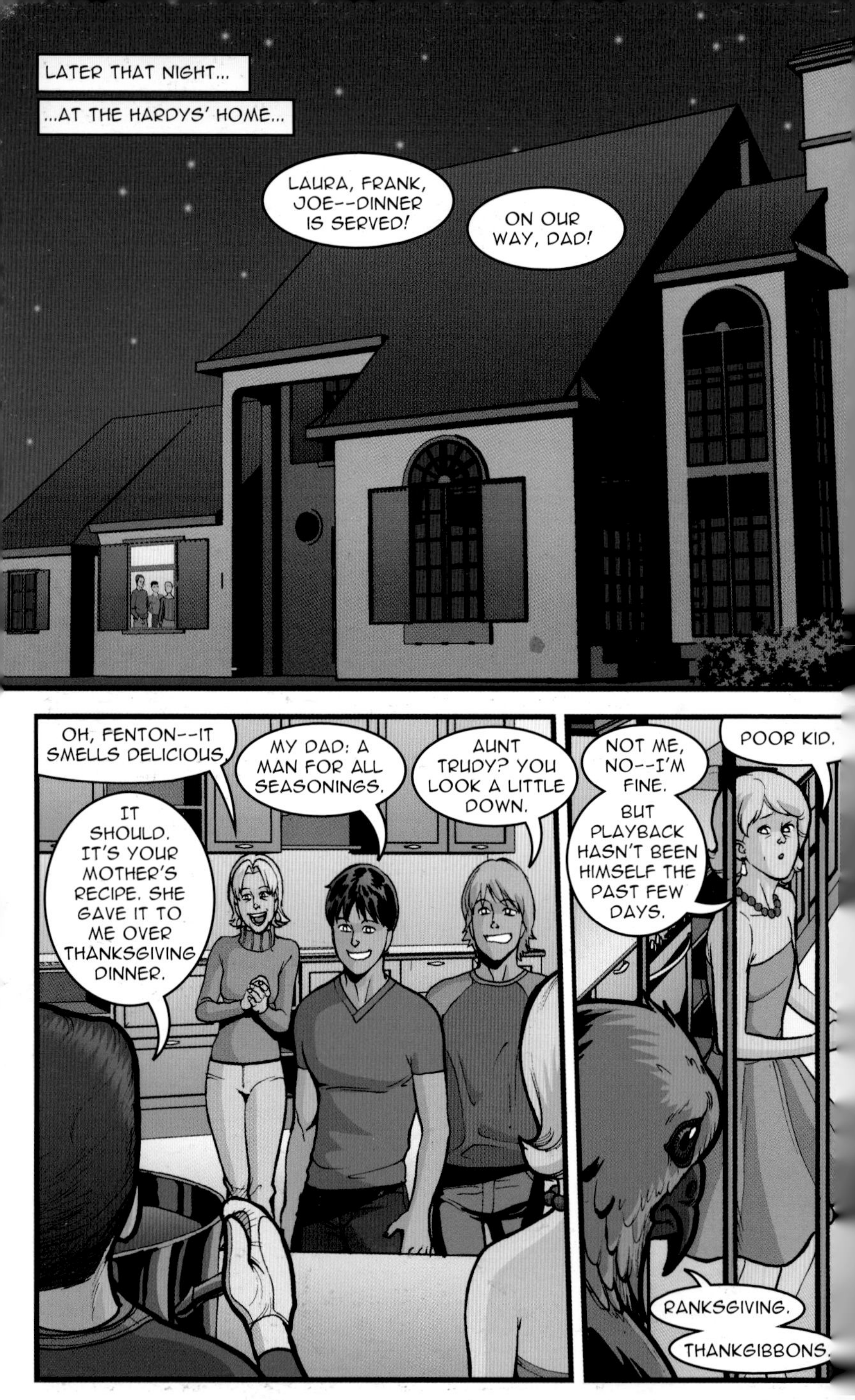
LATER THAT NIGHT...
...AT THE HARDYS' HOME...
LAURA, FRANK, JOE--DINNER IS SERVED!
ON OUR WAY, DAD!
OH, FENTON--IT SMELLS DELICIOUS.
IT SHOULD. IT'S YOUR MOTHER'S RECIPE. SHE GAVE IT TO ME OVER THANKSGIVING DINNER.
MY DAD: A MAN FOR ALL SEASONINGS.
AUNT TRUDY? YOU LOOK A LITTLE DOWN.
NOT ME, NO--I'M FINE.
BUT PLAYBACK HASN'T BEEN HIMSELF THE PAST FEW DAYS.
POOR KID.
RANKSGIVING.
THANKGIBBONS.

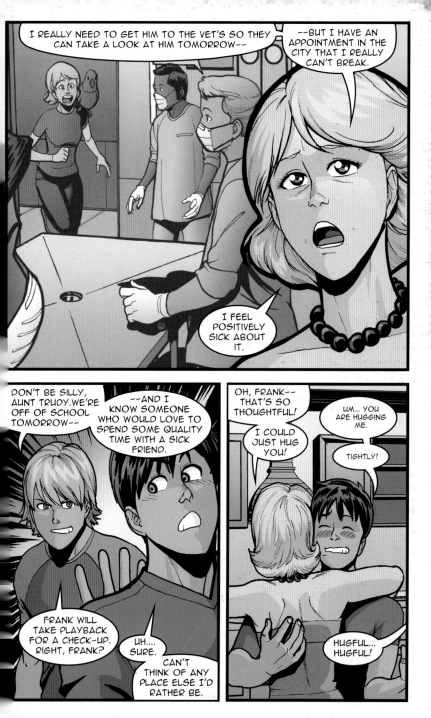

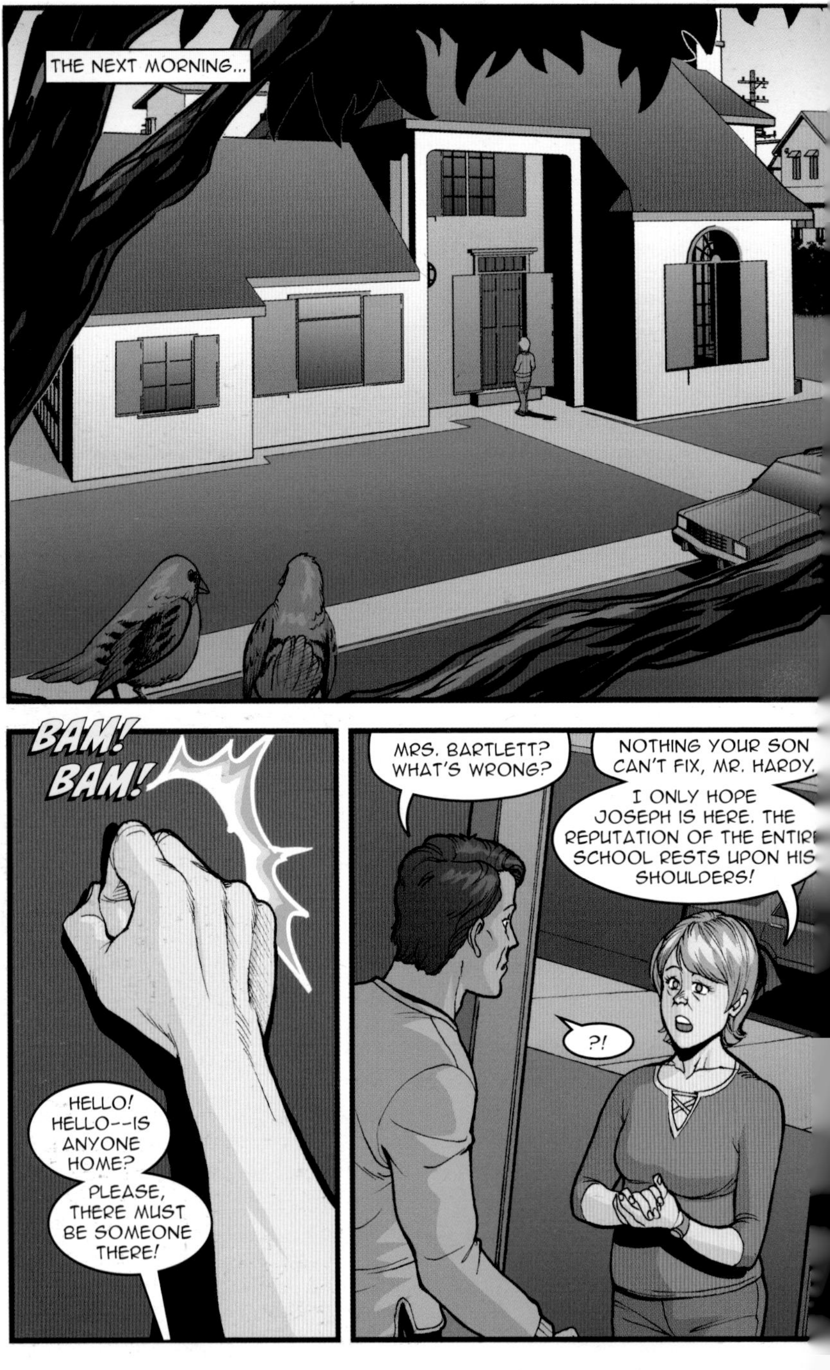
THE NEXT MORNING...
BAM! BAM!
HELLO! HELLO--IS ANYONE HOME?
PLEASE, THERE MUST BE SOMEONE THERE!
MRS. BARTLETT? WHAT'S WRONG?
?!
NOTHING YOUR SON CAN'T FIX, MR. HARDY.
I ONLY HOPE JOSEPH IS HERE. THE REPUTATION OF THE ENTIRE SCHOOL RESTS UPON HIS SHOULDERS!

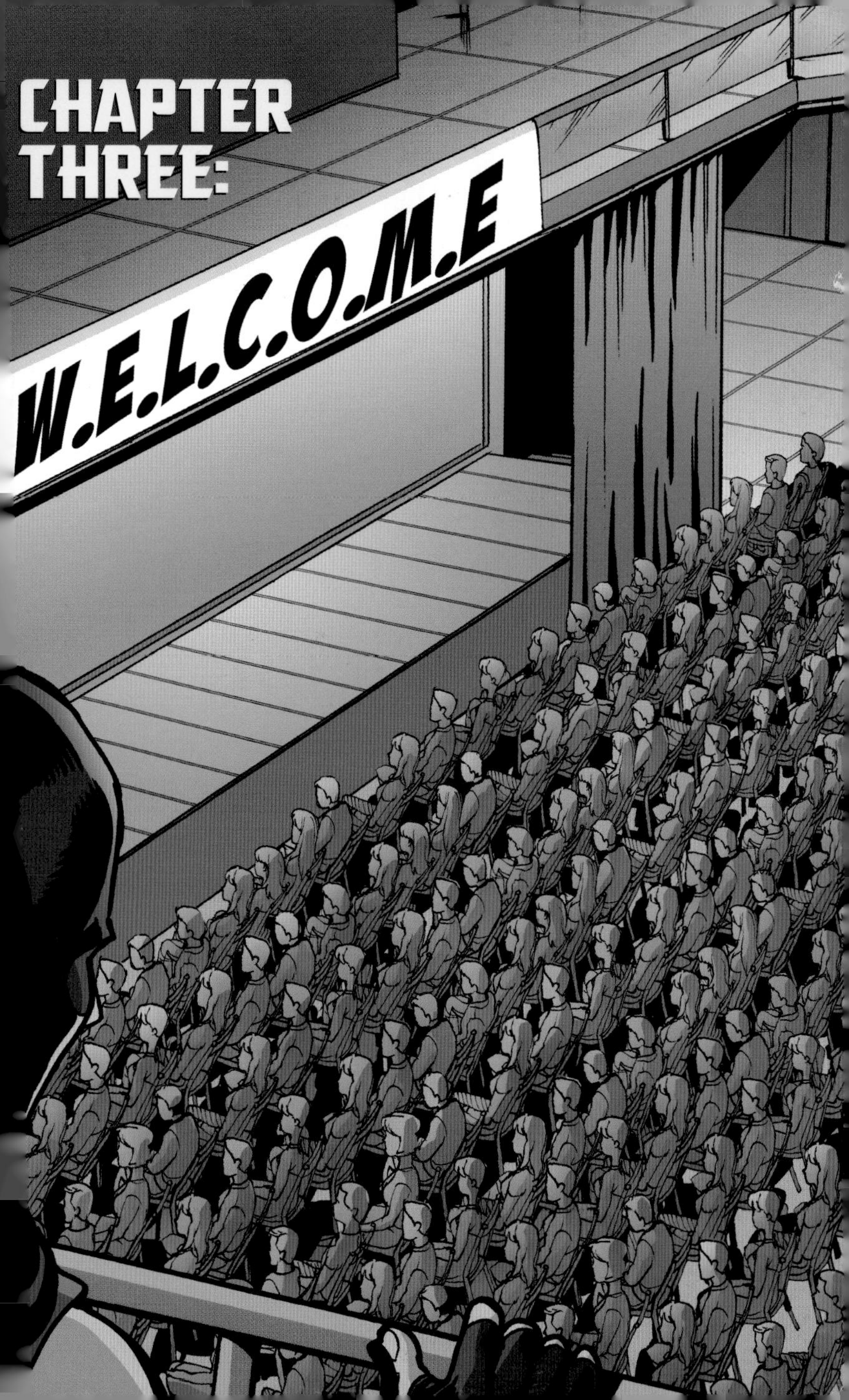
CHAPTER THREE:
W.E.L.C.O.M.E

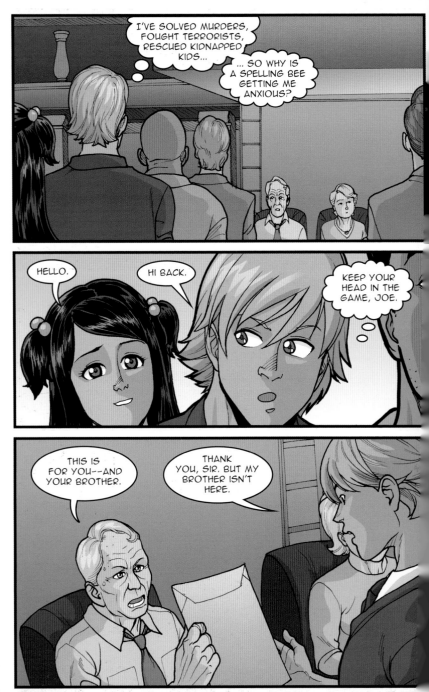

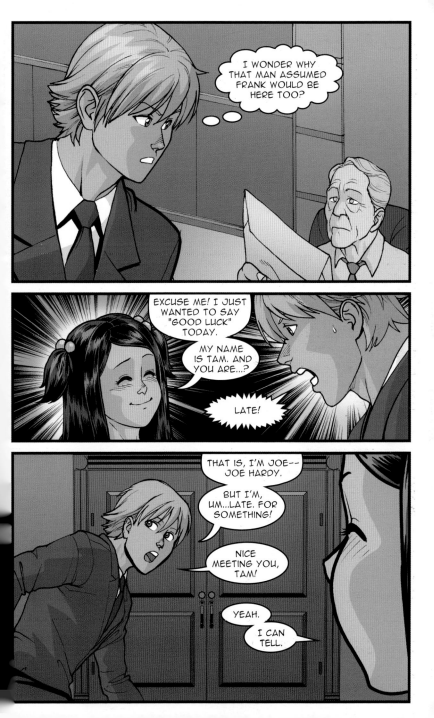

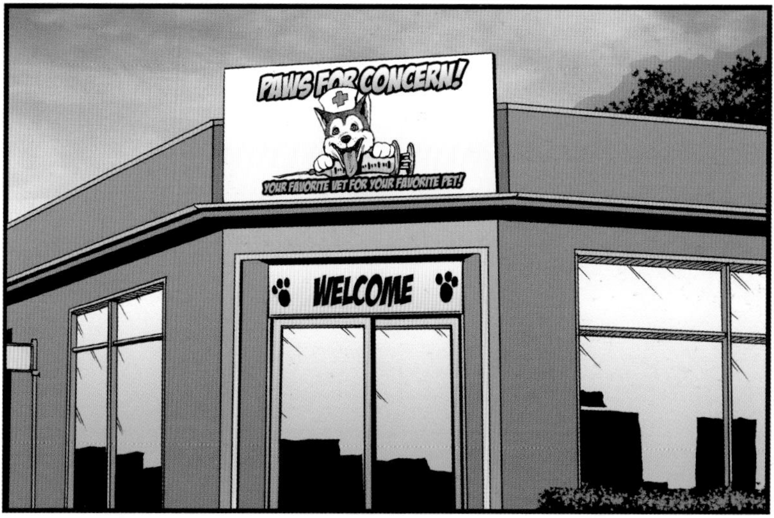
PAWS FOR CONCERN!
YOUR FAVORITE VET FOR YOUR FAVORITE PET!
WELCOME

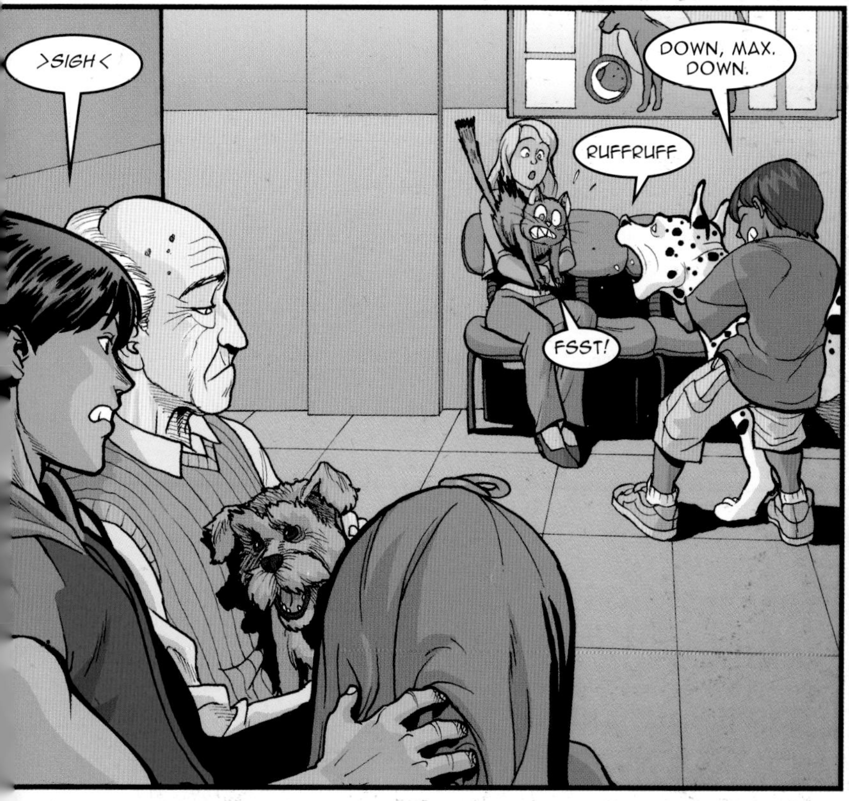
>SIGH<
DOWN, MAX. DOWN.
RUFFRUFF
FSST!

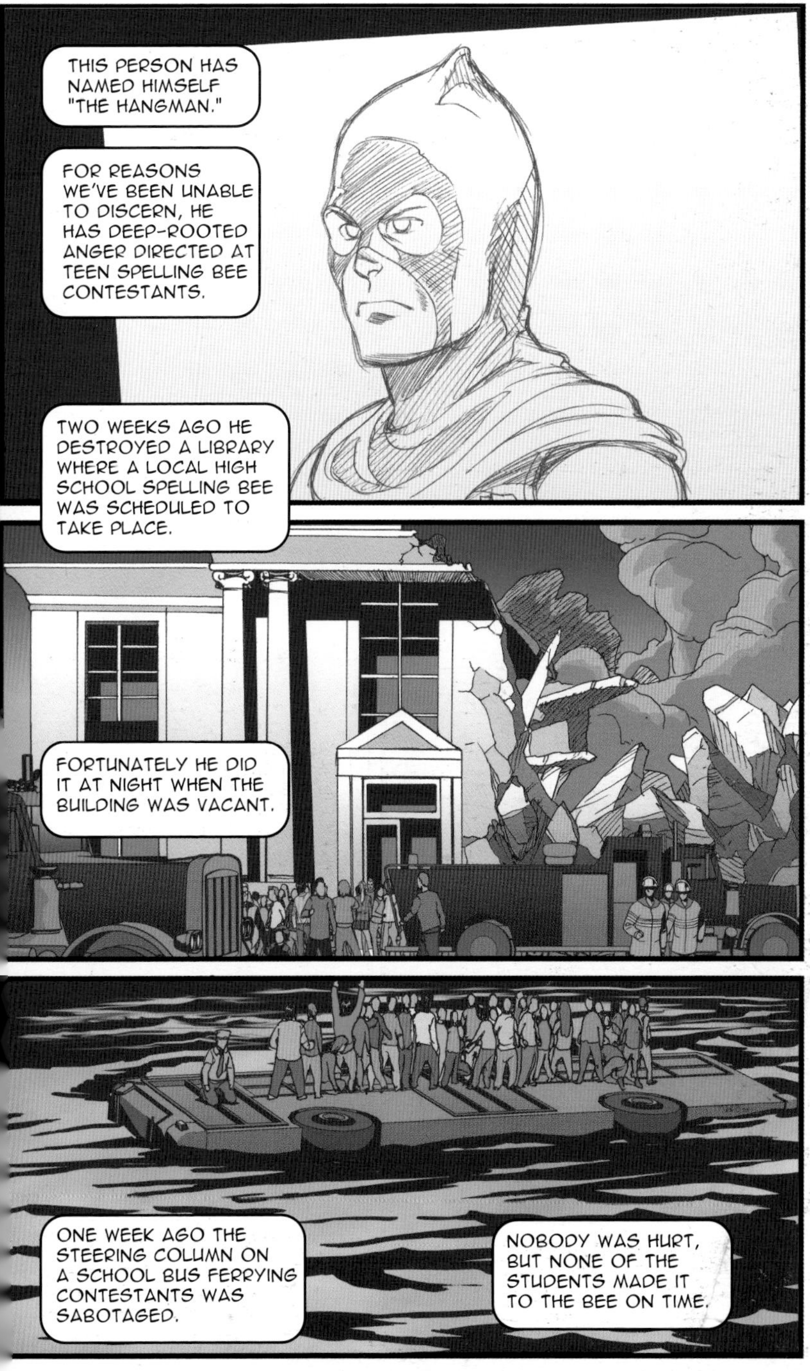
THIS PERSON HAS NAMED HIMSELF "THE HANGMAN."
FOR REASONS WE'VE BEEN UNABLE TO DISCERN, HE HAS DEEP-ROOTED ANGER DIRECTED AT TEEN SPELLING BEE CONTESTANTS.
TWO WEEKS AGO HE DESTROYED A LIBRARY WHERE A LOCAL HIGH SCHOOL SPELLING BEE WAS SCHEDULED TO TAKE PLACE.
FORTUNATELY HE DID IT AT NIGHT WHEN THE BUILDING WAS VACANT.
ONE WEEK AGO THE STEERING COLUMN ON A SCHOOL BUS FERRYING CONTESTANTS WAS SABOTAGED.
NOBODY WAS HURT, BUT NONE OF THE STUDENTS MADE IT TO THE BEE ON TIME.

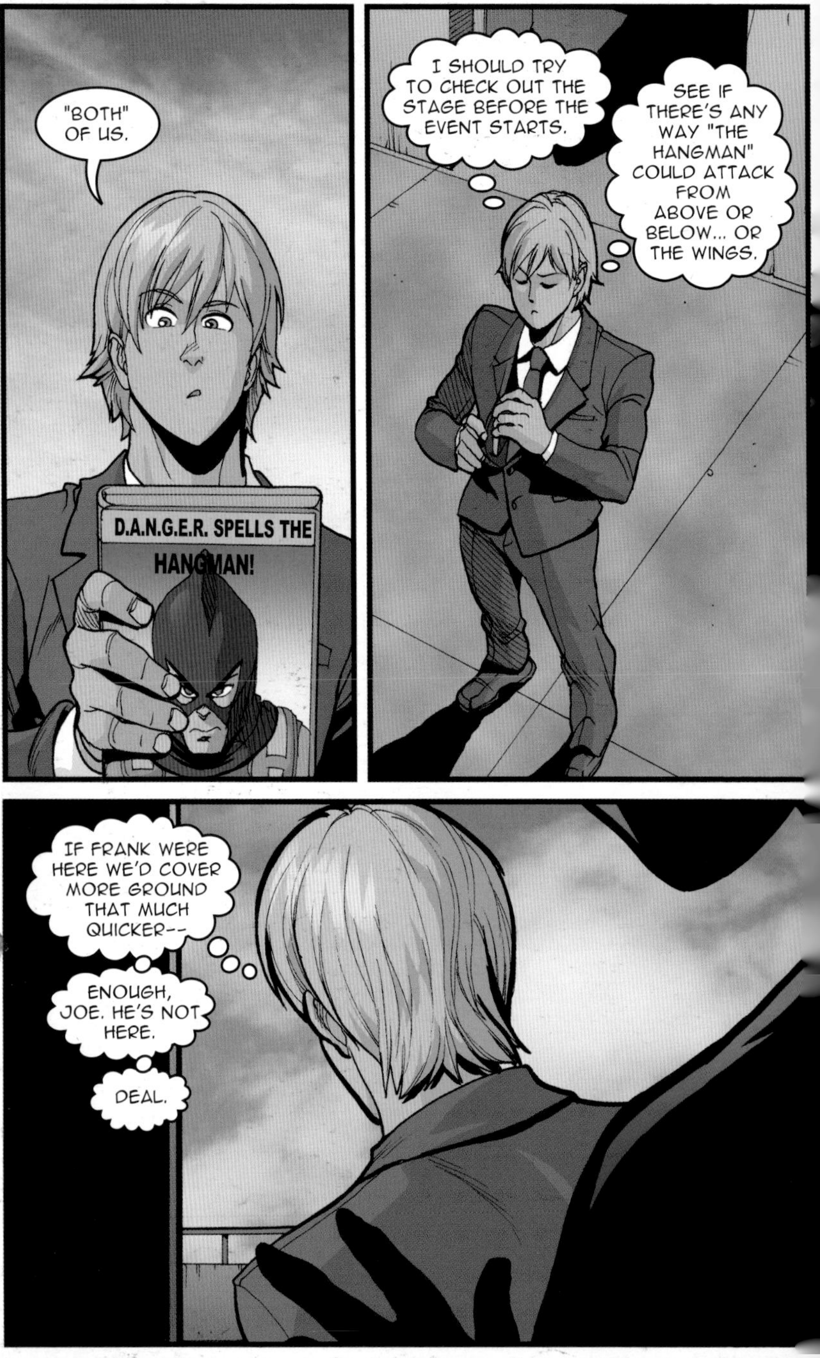
"BOTH" OF US.
D.A.N.G.E.R. SPELLS THE HANGMAN!
I SHOULD TRY TO CHECK OUT THE STAGE BEFORE THE EVENT STARTS.
SEE IF THERE'S ANY WAY "THE HANGMAN" COULD ATTACK FROM ABOVE OR BELOW... OR THE WINGS.
IF FRANK WERE HERE WE'D COVER MORE GROUND THAT MUCH QUICKER--
ENOUGH, JOE. HE'S NOT HERE.
DEAL.

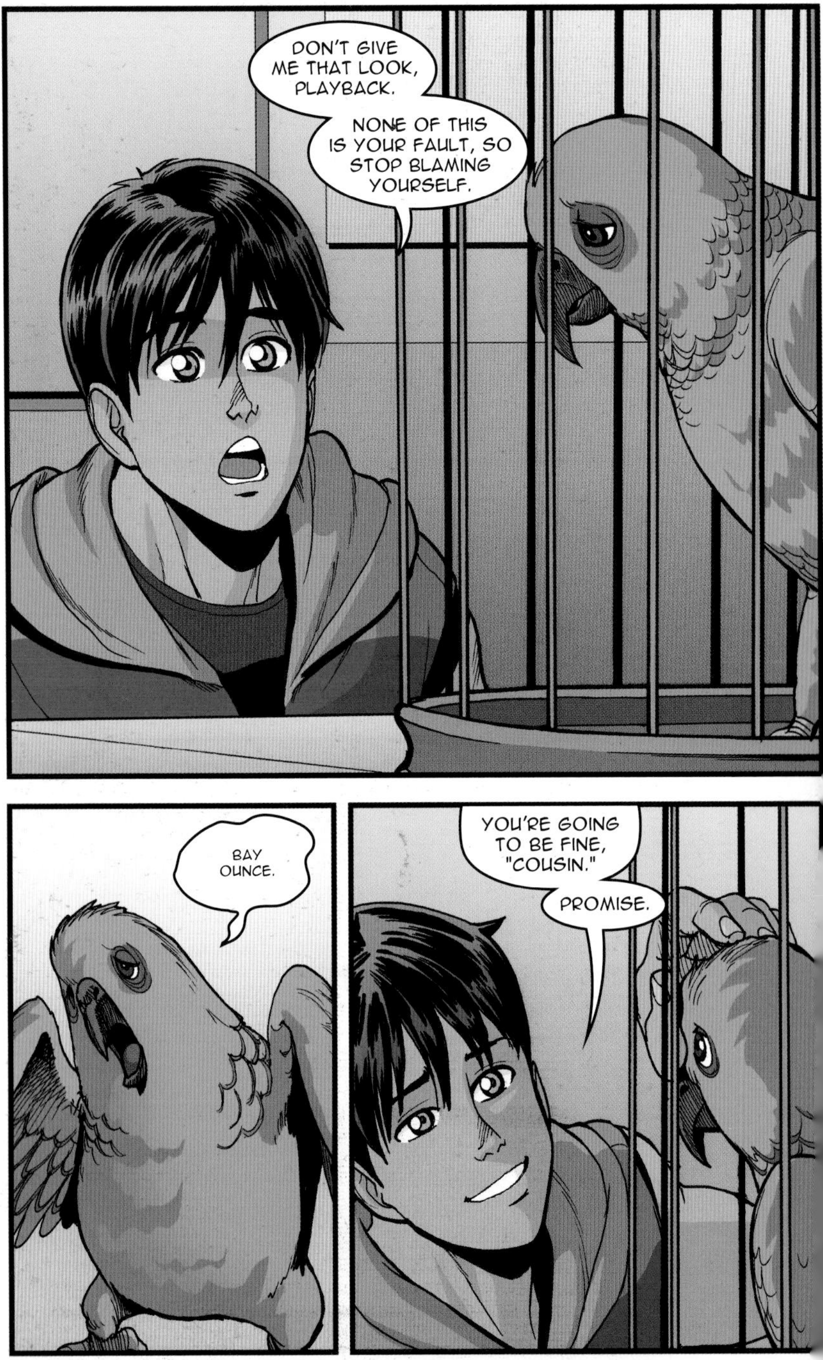
DON'T GIVE ME THAT LOOK, PLAYBACK.
NONE OF THIS IS YOUR FAULT, SO STOP BLAMING YOURSELF.
BAY OUNCE.
YOU'RE GOING TO BE FINE, "COUSIN."
PROMISE.

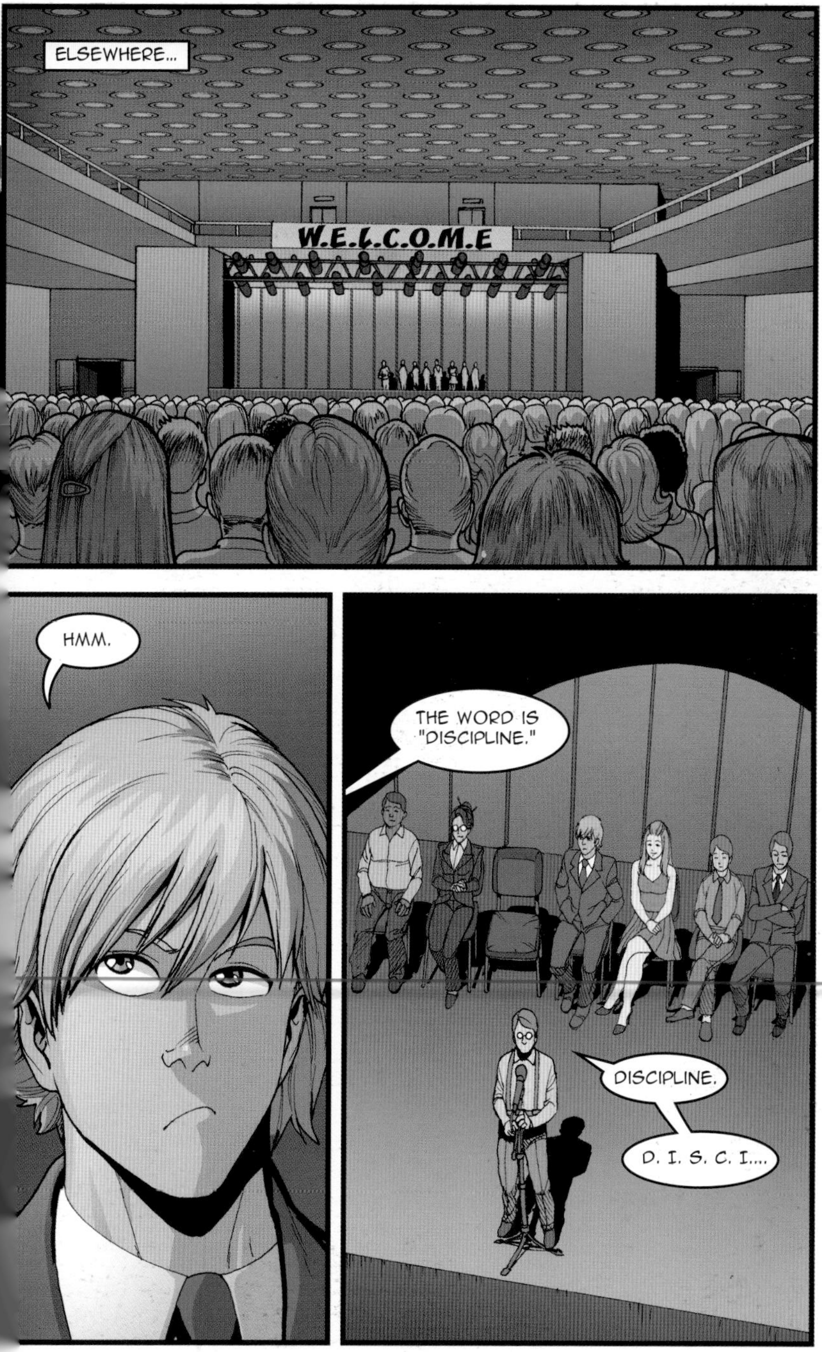
ELSEWHERE...
W.E.L.C.O.M.E
HMM.
THE WORD IS "DISCIPLINE."
DISCIPLINE.
D. I. S. C. I....

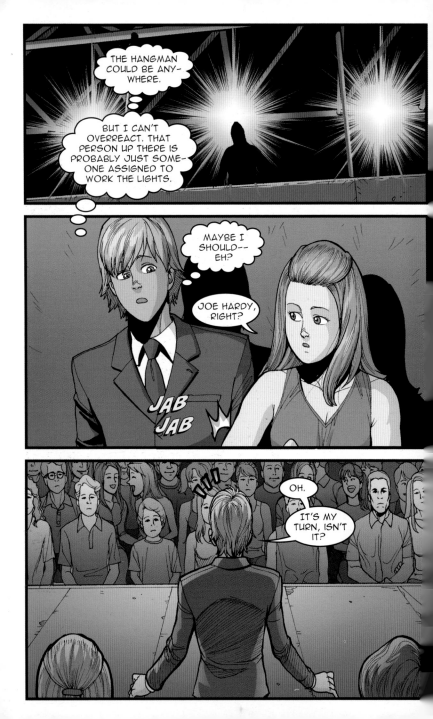

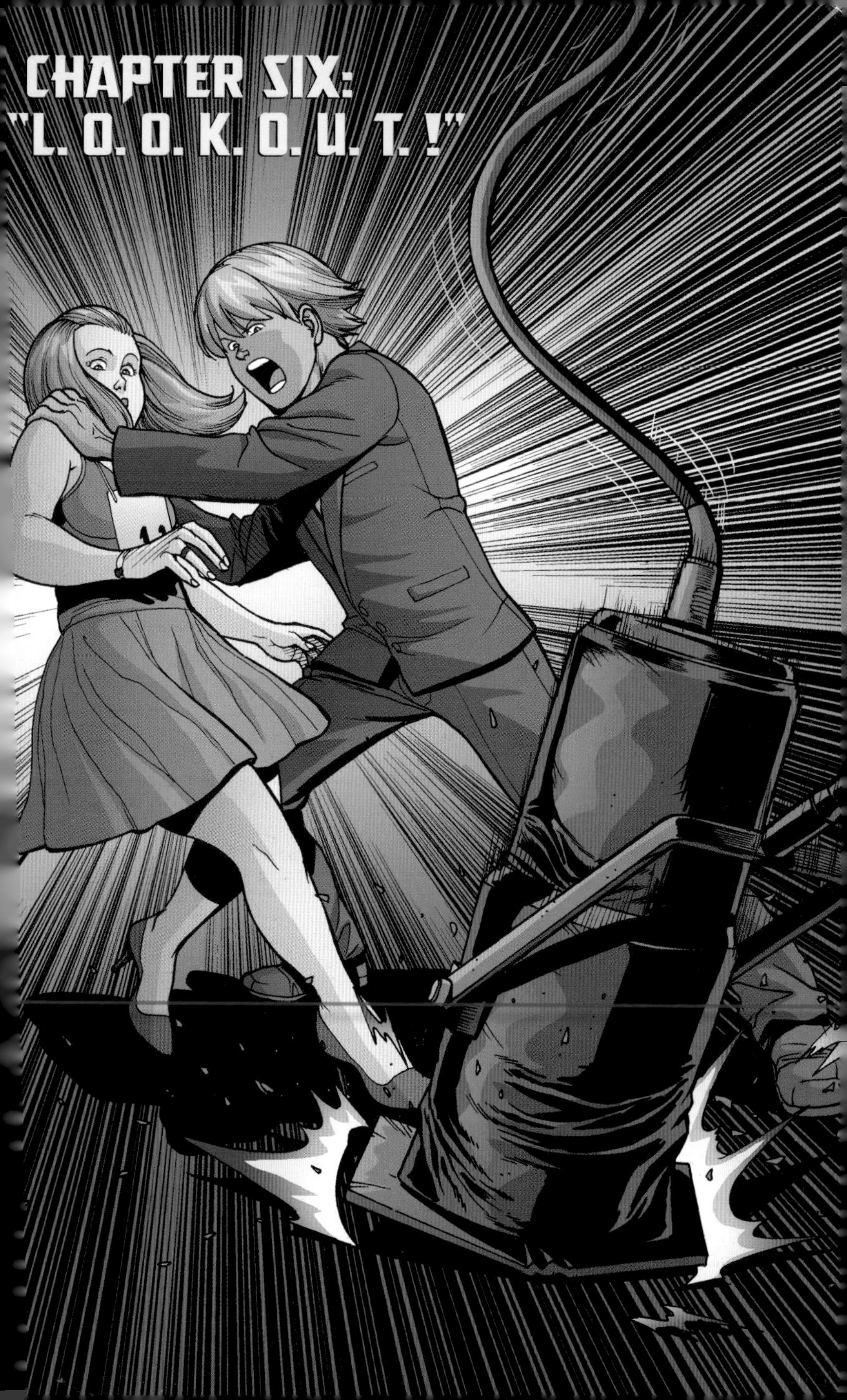
CHAPTER SIX:
"L. O. O. K. O. U. T. !"

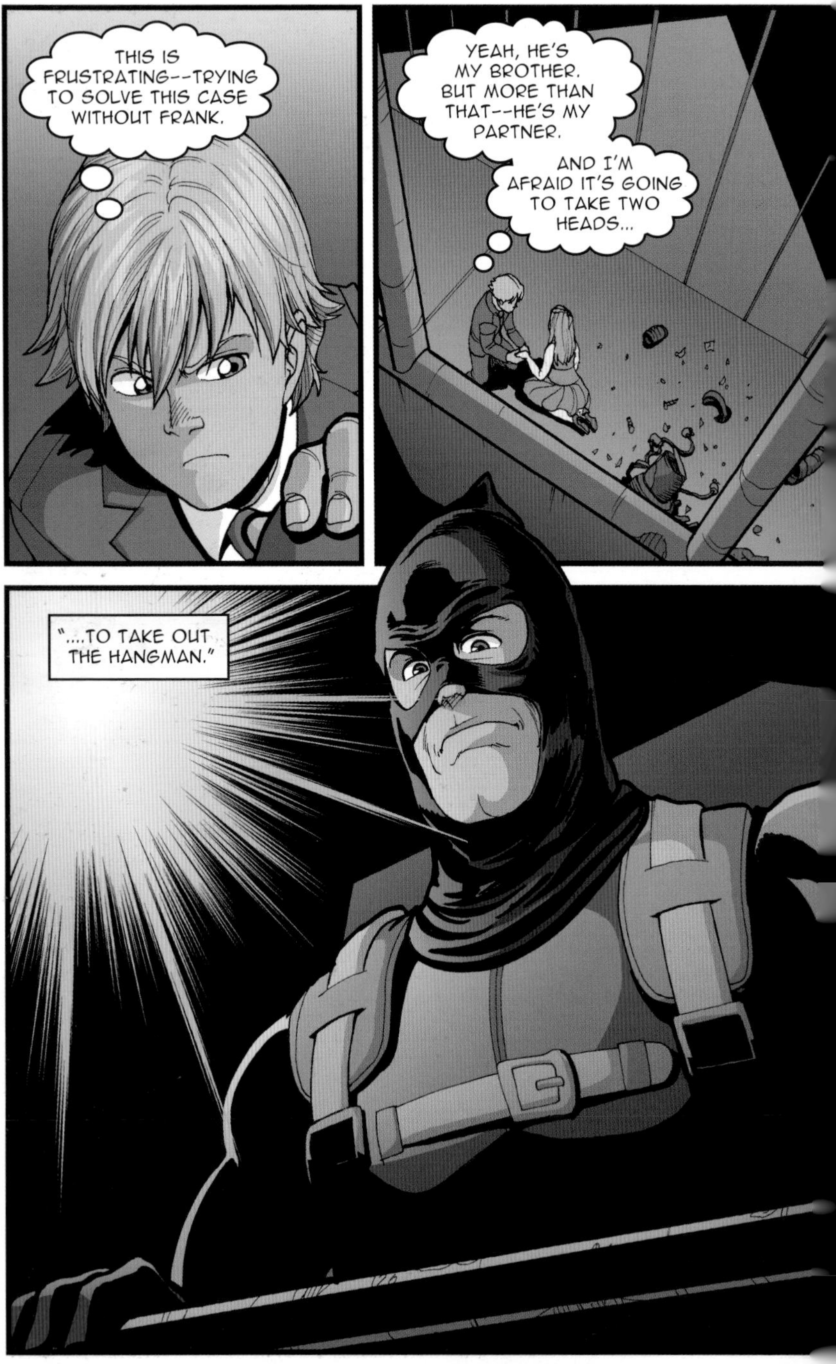
THIS IS FRUSTRATING--TRYING TO SOLVE THIS CASE WITHOUT FRANK.
YEAH, HE'S MY BROTHER. BUT MORE THAN THAT--HE'S MY PARTNER.
AND I'M AFRAID IT'S GOING TO TAKE TWO HEADS...
"....TO TAKE OUT THE HANGMAN."

CHAPTER SEVEN: "I BEFORE E... ESPECIALLY AFTER DIE!"

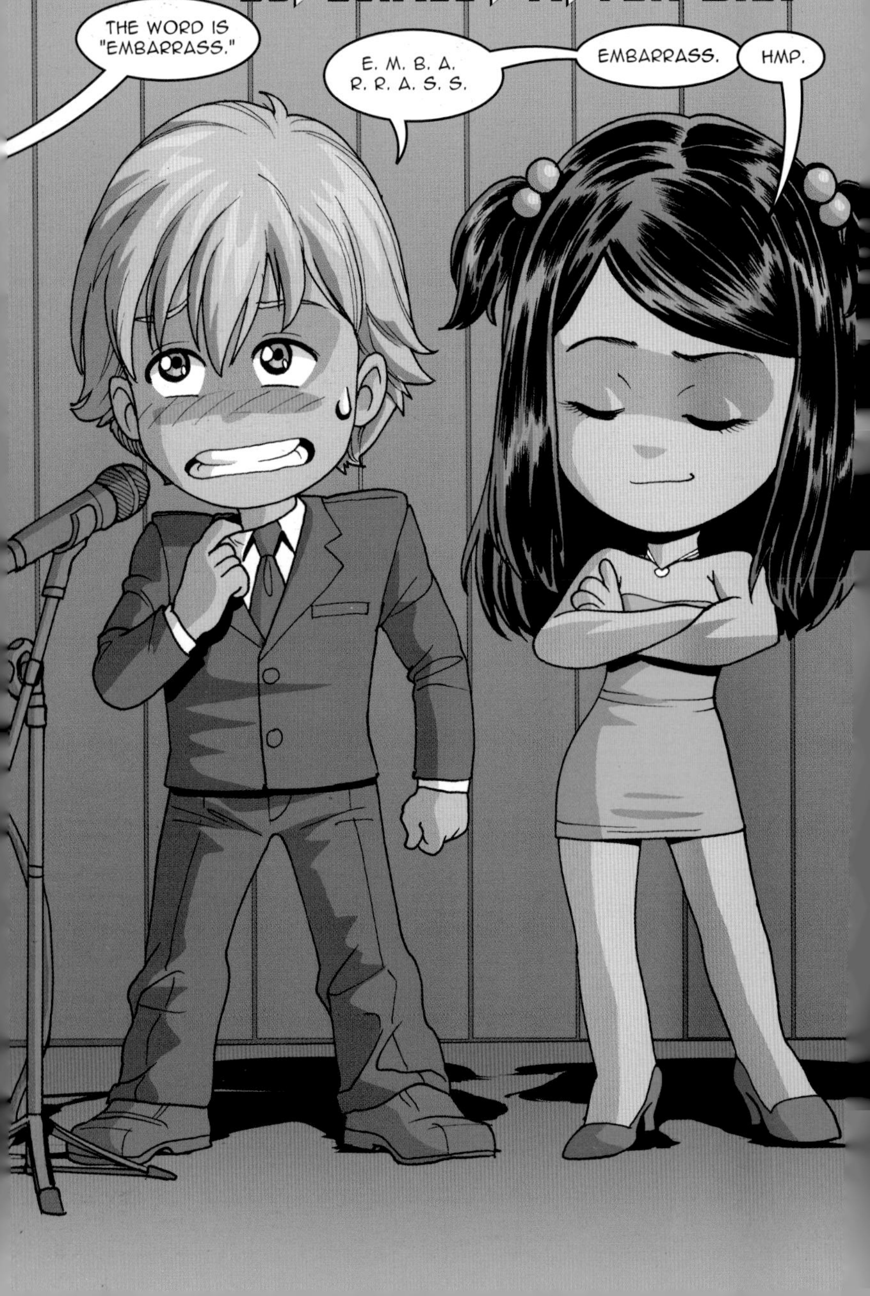
THE WORD IS "EMBARRASS."
E. M. B. A. R. R. A. S. S.
EMBARRASS.
HMP.

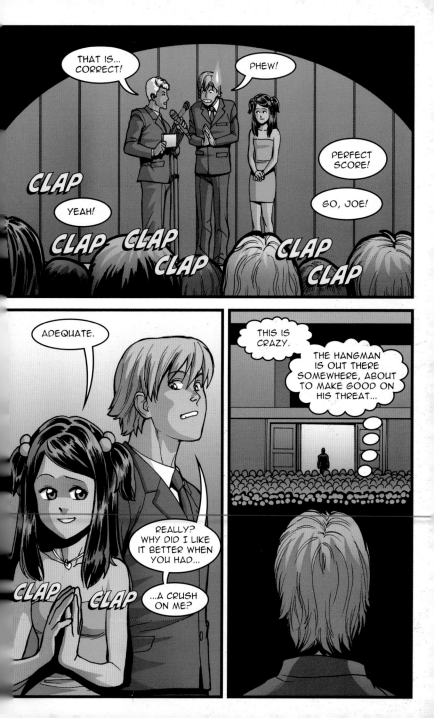

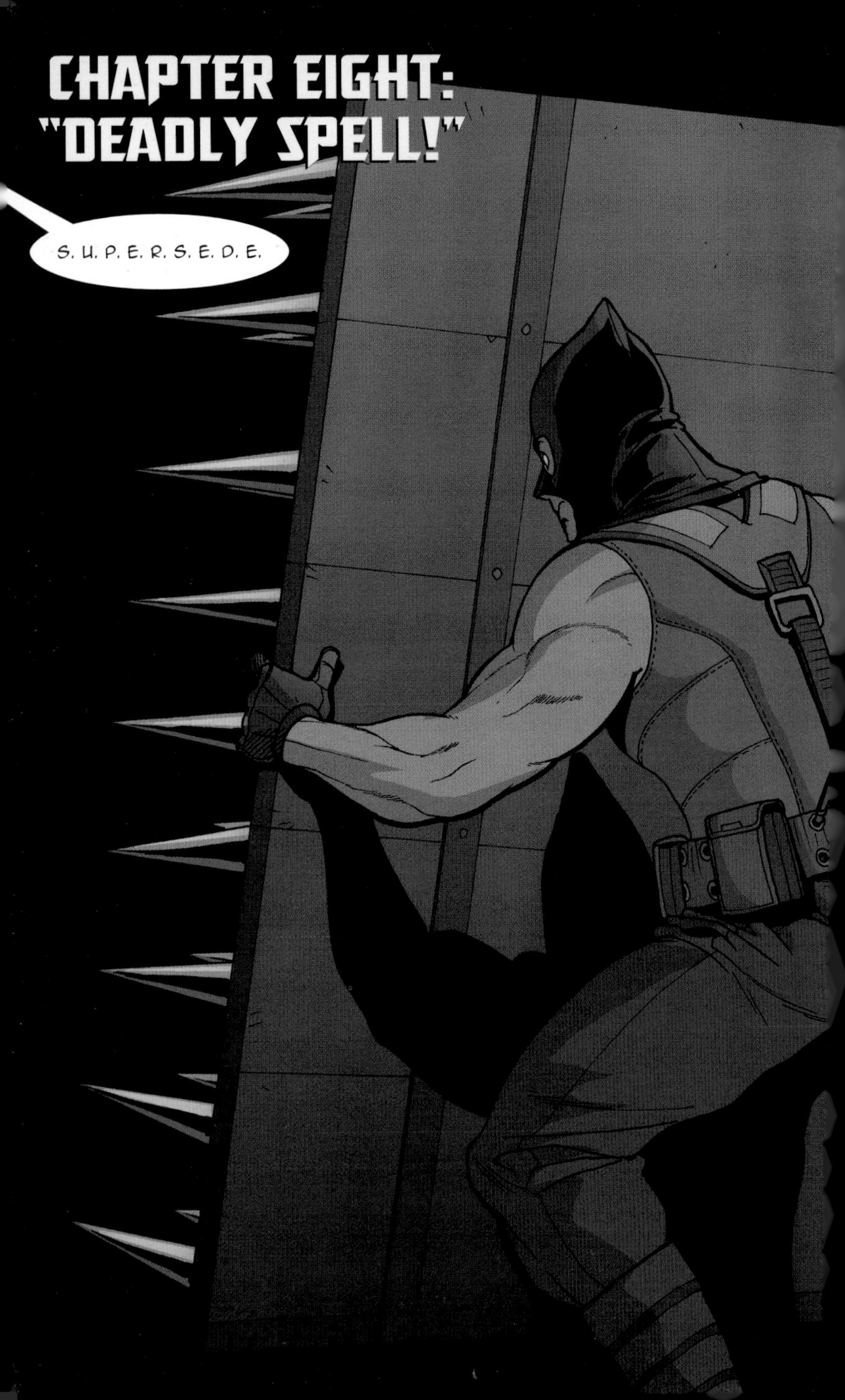
CHAPTER EIGHT:
"DEADLY SPELL!"
S. U. P. E. R. S. E. D. E.

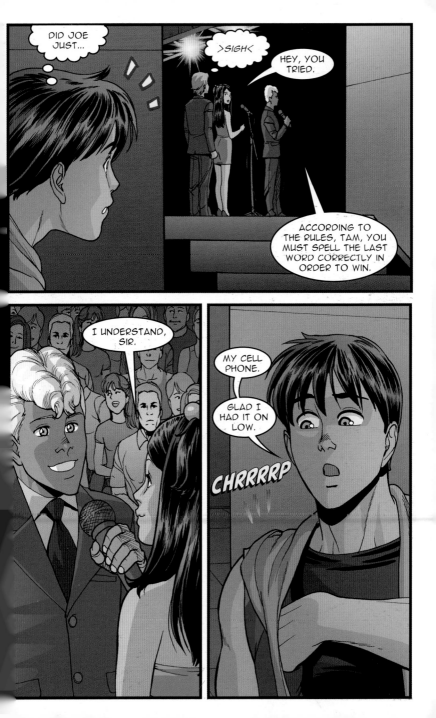

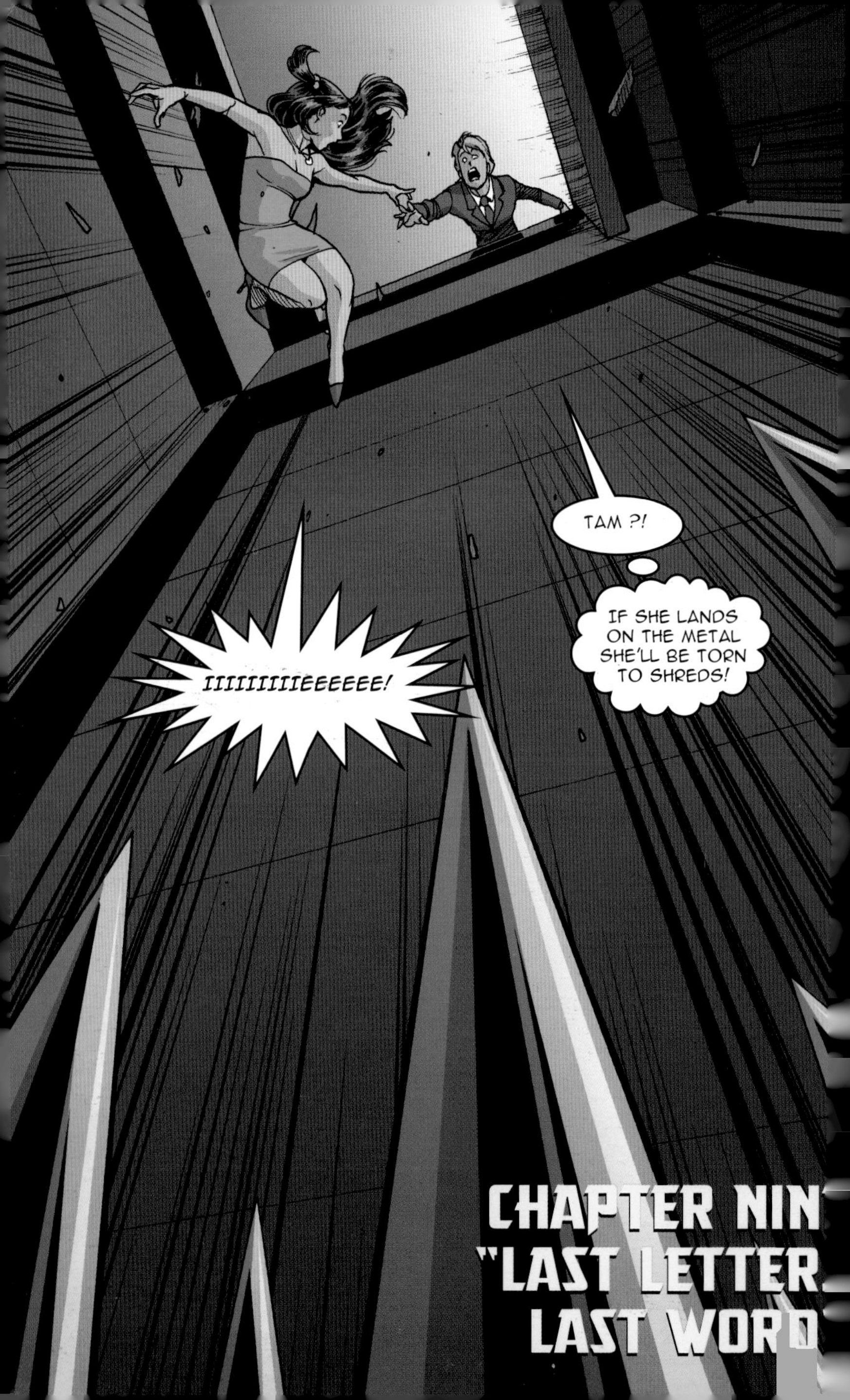
TAM ?!
IIIIIIIIIEEEEEE!
IF SHE LANDS ON THE METAL SHE'LL BE TORN TO SHREDS!
CHAPTER NIN
"LAST LETTER
LAST WORD

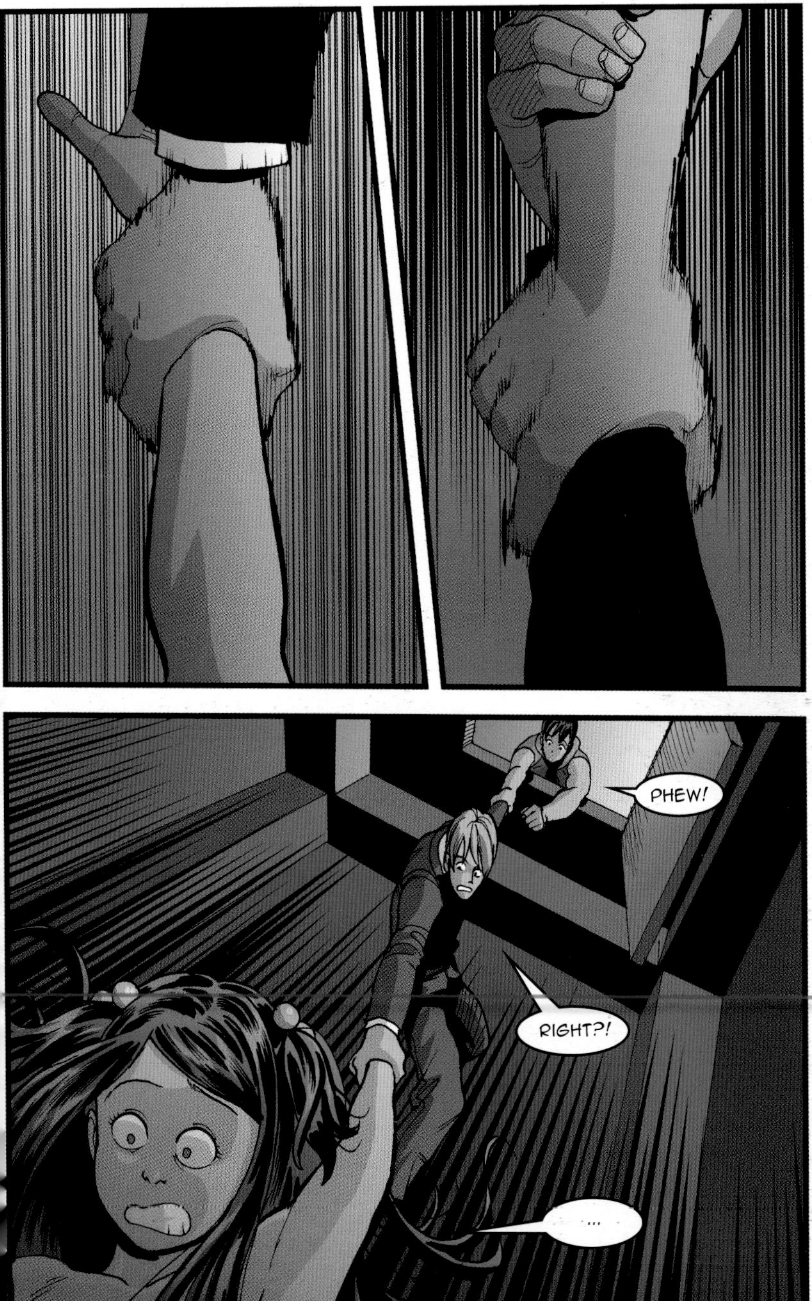
PHEW!
RIGHT?!
...

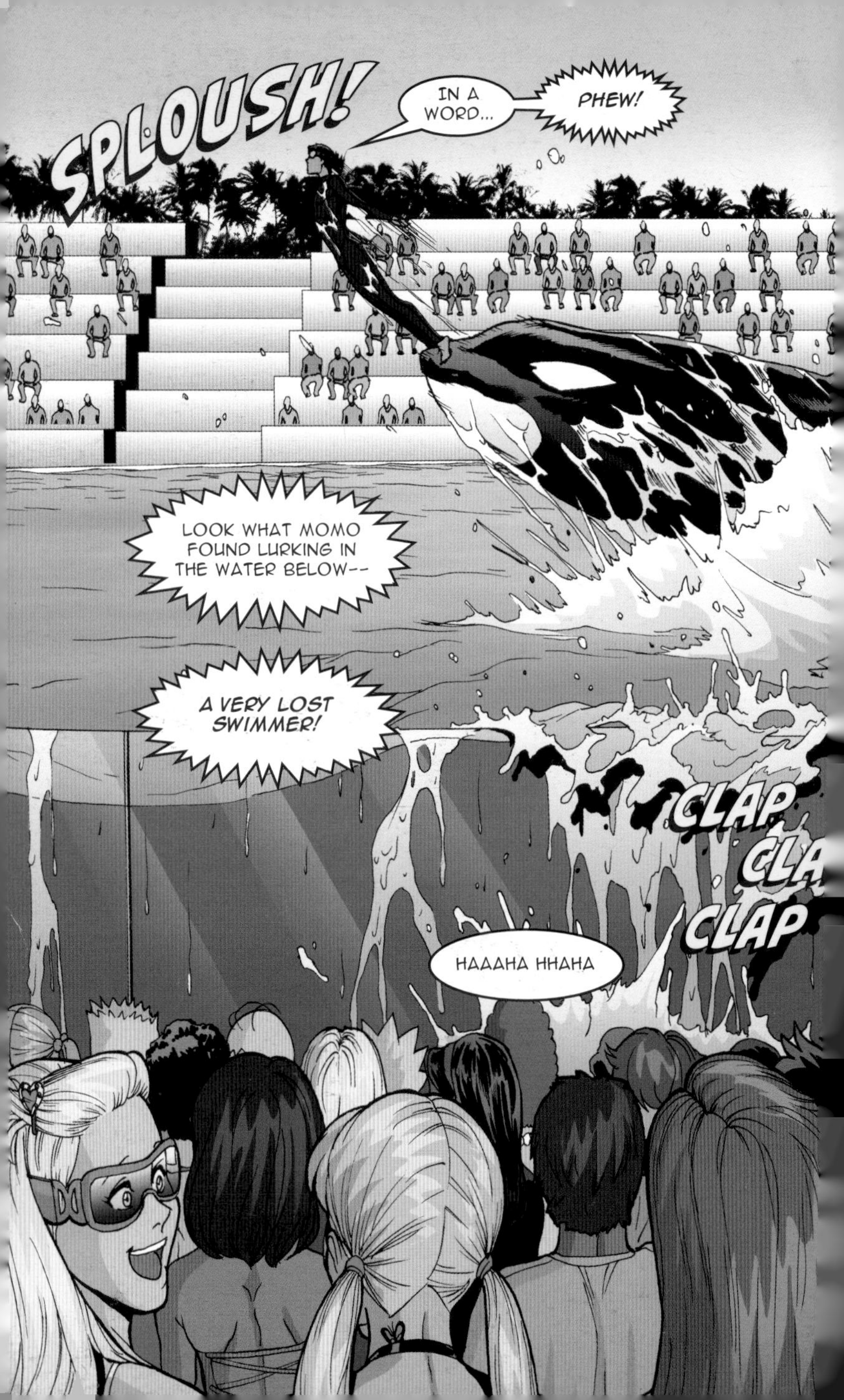
SPLOUSH!
IN A WORD...
PHEW!
LOOK WHAT MOMO FOUND LURKING IN THE WATER BELOW--
A VERY LOST SWIMMER!
CLAP CLA CLAP
HAAAHA HHAHA

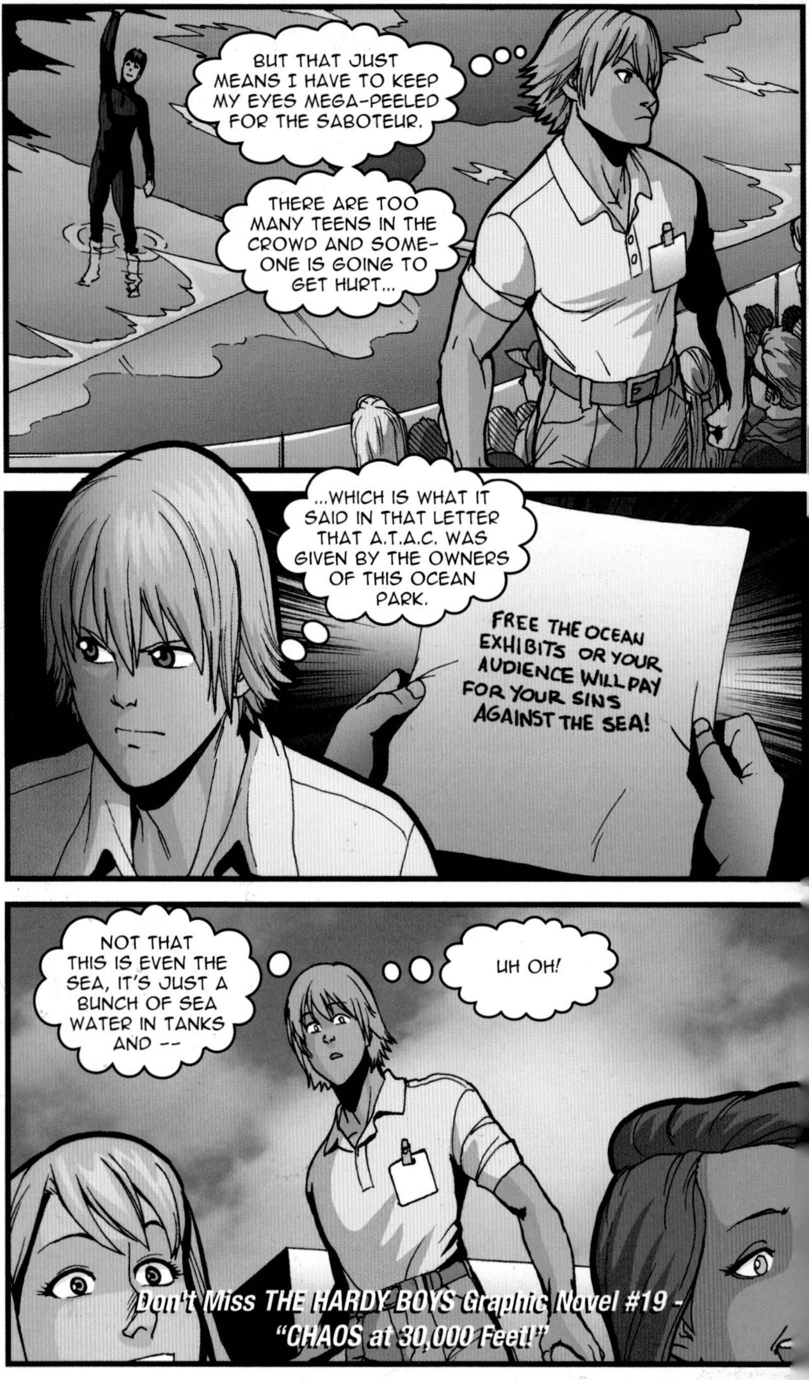
BUT THAT JUST MEANS I HAVE TO KEEP MY EYES MEGA-PEELED FOR THE SABOTEUR.
THERE ARE TOO MANY TEENS IN THE CROWD AND SOME-ONE IS GOING TO GET HURT...
...WHICH IS WHAT IT SAID IN THAT LETTER THAT A.T.A.C. WAS GIVEN BY THE OWNERS OF THIS OCEAN PARK.
FREE THE OCEAN EXHIBITS OR YOUR AUDIENCE WILL PAY FOR YOUR SINS AGAINST THE SEA!
NOT THAT THIS IS EVEN THE SEA, IT'S JUST A BUNCH OF SEA WATER IN TANKS AND --
UH OH!
Don't Miss THE HARDY BOYS Graphic Novel #19 - "CHAOS at 30,000 Feet!"

WATCH OUT FOR PAPERCUTZ™

For long-time followers of THE HARDY BOYS Graphic Novels, I don't need to tell you that this little section of the book is called the Papercutz Backpages – the place to find out all sorts of things about all your favorite Papercutz titles and creators. But if this particular HARDY BOYS Graphic Novel is your very first Papercutz experience, then welcome! I'm Jim Salicrup, the lucky guy who happens to be the Editor-in-Chief of this wonderful little comics and graphic novels–creating company.

Not only do we bring you all-new exciting HARDY BOYS graphic novels every three months, but we also publish all-new graphic novels starring NANCY DREW, BIONICLE, and TALES FROM THE CRYPT. We also bring you comics adaptations of Stories by the World's Greatest Authors in CLASSICS ILLUSTRATED and CLASSICS ILLUSTRATED DELUXE. We also have a new series of graphic novels starring a time-traveling mouse named GERONIMO STILTON, who is saving the future, by protecting the past. We have another all-new series coming your way, but let's keep that a secret for just a little longer.

Of course, the very best way to get the most up-to-date Papercutz news and information is to visit our website at www.papercutz.com. Perhaps the most popular feature on there is our Papercutz Blog, featuring posts by such Papercutz super-stars as Scott Lobdell, Paulo Henrique, Stefan Petrucha, Sarah Kinney, Sho Murase, Greg Farshtey, and Michael Petranek! The stuff on the Blog is so great, we'll be running some of the best bits here as well. For example, the Papercutz Profile on THE HARDY BOYS artist Paulo Henrique (or "PH" as he prefers) originally appeared online, but we added some more art and photos, and are running it at the end of this edition of the Papercutz Backpages.

But that's not all! We also have a special preview of perhaps the most eagerly awaited edition of TALES FROM THE CRYPT -- #8 "Diary of a Stinky Dead Kid." We think the cover may give you a clue why…

To get just a small sample of what all the fuss is about, check out the preview on the next few pages!

So, enjoy the Paulo profile, the Papercutz Blog, and the CRYPT preview – and don't forget, we'll be back soon in HARDY BOYS Graphic Novel #19 when you'll need to buckle your safety belt to survive "Chaos at 30,000 Feet!"

Thanks,

Jim

October
Monday

My name's Glugg. It's always sad and scary when a kid dies, especially if it's you. Funny, for the longest time I thought the scariest thing was my brother, Rock.

He's twice my size and only has room in his brain for his band, bullying me and making fun of this journal. I think he's jealous I can write. Plus he wants a new drum set badly, and our parents made it clear we can't afford one.

Anyway, it turns out there ARE things scarier than Rock, just a couple, though, like death.

Have you ever just KNOWN the phone will ring and exactly who's calling and you feel really cool, like it's magic or something?

You'd think with something big as DEATH, you'd get the same kind of warning, but nope. Not me, anyway. No bells, no whistles, not even a vague sense of impending doom.

It sucks! I mean I was minding my own business, standing next to my pal Al Crowley at the train station with the rest of the kids, on our dumb school trip to the Museum, when...

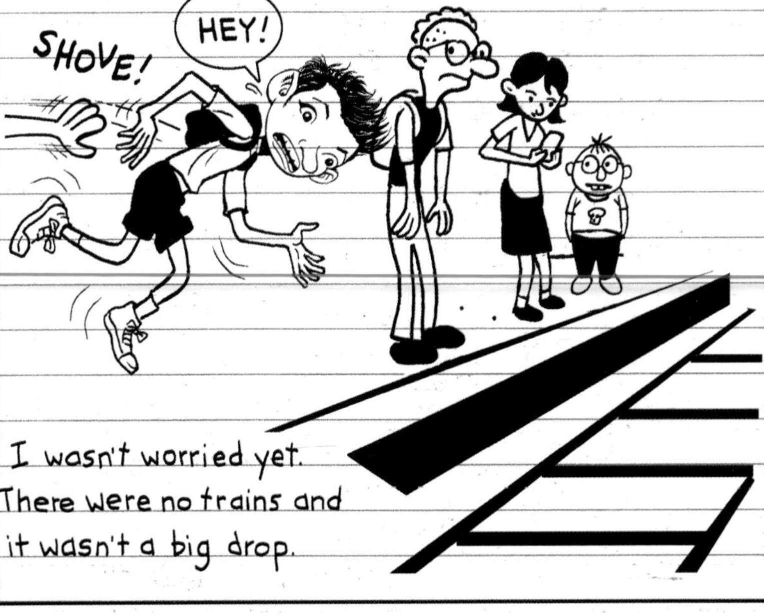
SHOVE!
HEY!

I wasn't worried yet. There were no trains and it wasn't a big drop.

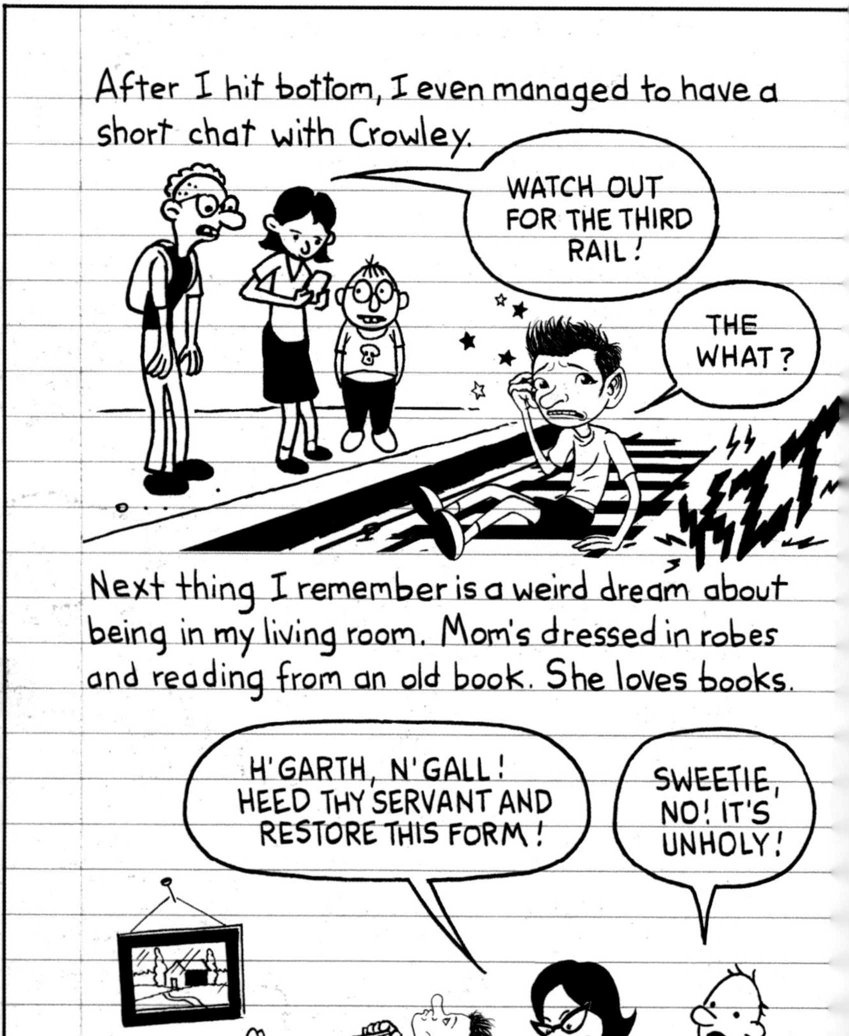
After I hit bottom, I even managed to have a short chat with Crowley.
WATCH OUT FOR THE THIRD RAIL!
THE WHAT?
Next thing I remember is a weird dream about being in my living room. Mom's dressed in robes and reading from an old book. She loves books.
H'GARTH, N'GALL! HEED THY SERVANT AND RESTORE THIS FORM!
SWEETIE, NO! IT'S UNHOLY!

Don't miss TALES FROM THE CRYPT # 8 "Diary of a Stinky Dead Kid"!

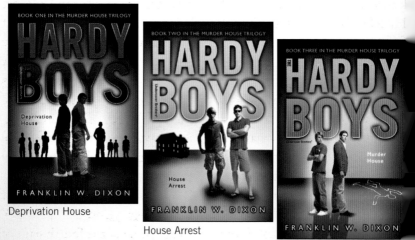

MEET HARDY BOYS GRAPHIC NOVELS ARTIST "PH"-
PAULO HENRIQUE!

— A **PAPERCUTZ** PROFILE —

Hi there, my name is Paulo Henrique and most of you know me as the artist of THE HARDY BOYS Graphic Novels for Papercutz. One thing you might not know is that I prefer to go by "PH" instead of "Paulo Henrique." I'd like to share a bit about myself and let you all ask any questions you may have for me over on the Papercutz Blog (go to www.papercutz.com). I always like to hear from fans.

I was born in Sao Paulo, Brazil where I started drawing at very young age. The first thing I remember drawing was from

when I was 6 years old. I was in art class and I drew a picture of Darth Vader – the villain from STAR WARS. The teacher said she thought that I had drawn a bride in a black wedding dress! I always liked bad guys the best, but I knew that Vader was a good guy under that mask. That's why I liked him so much as a kid.

After that, I just kept on drawing and drawing. I really like "larger than life" characters, and when I was growing up I was drawn to Manga-style art before I even knew that's what it was called. Manga is actually the Japanese word for comics, but there are many unique elements of this Japanese art style that we use in THE HARDY BOYS a lot. An easy way to identify the style is characters with cartoonishly exaggerated faces and bodies. If you want a good example of some Manga-esque HARDY BOYS, look at the fourth page of comics in THE HARDY BOYS Graphic Novel #14 "Haley Danielle's Top Eight!":

Some of the best-known artists who shaped what we know as Manga today are Machiko Hasegawa and Osamu Tezuka. You have probably seen Tezuka's "Astro Boy" at some point in your life. Google it! The history of Manga goes all the way back to the 1800's and there's a lot of info on the Internet if you do some searching.

Back to my art! Some of you may want to know who my favorite comics characters are and how I got started. Well, I love that Blue Bomber! I'm talking about Megaman.

I started drawing him when I was a teenager and I've beaten all of the original Nintendo games. Megaman is a Manga character and he jump-started my career. In 1997, I was hired to draw the MEGAMAN comicbook for Brazilian publisher Magnum and ended up working with Sidney Lima, who would work on ZORRO and THE HARDY BOYS at Papercutz years later. At that time, a lot of publishers got interested in Manga, so I met with Magnum and did a test for Megaman. Both Sidney Lima and I ended up getting the job and we became friends.

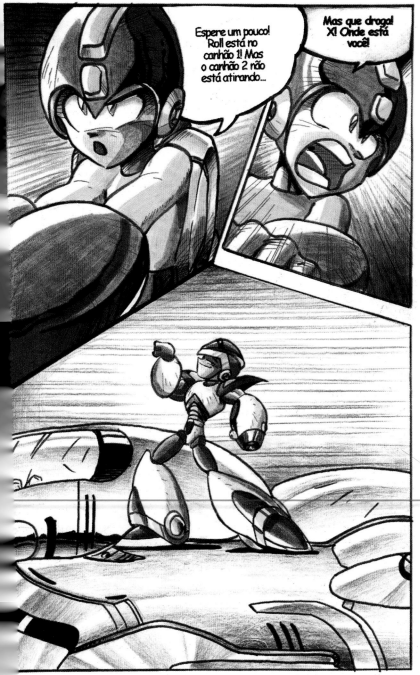

Years later I started to work for Yabu Media and was doing an electronic graphic novel called COMBO RANGERS, so I called him to work with me. This led to us collaborating on THE HARDY BOYS. He is a good friend and a great artist. I have to thank him for introducing me to Papercutz and THE HARDY BOYS. The MEGAMAN series took off, and I ended up teaching Manga-style drawing to young artists at a place called Impacto Studios in Brazil.

Combo Rangers Revolution © 2000 Yabu Media

Impacto Studios is a place where young artists can come to learn and improve their art, while more established artists teach classes to students and are introduced to companies that may want to hire them. At Impacto, I became friends with Klebs Junior, the founder of the studio and a comicbook artist himself. Klebs is well-known in comics. Aside from founding Impacto he also illustrated SNAKES ON A PLANE (DC), EXCALIBUR (Marvel Comics), HARBINGER and a bunch of other titles. Klebs became my agent and helped get my work to America. When he heard that Top Cow Productions at Image Comics was looking for an artist for their MYTH WARRIORS series, he set up a test for me. Top Cow hired me and my work ended up getting distributed to a much larger audience in the US.

I worked for a lot of different magazines and publications in Brazil, but it wasn't until THE HARDY BOYS #6 "Hyde and Shriek" that I started working on that series. My friend Sidney needed some help. He asked me to help draw THE HARDY BOYS #6 and then I started drawing it full-time and have no plans to stop! I just finished my 12th volume of the series.

Aside from comics, I really love music. I have remixed a lot of Megaman songs from the

Paulo and his band "Octane" in THE HARDY BOYS 17 "Word Up!"

More art from Paulo's work on COMBO RANGER.

video games and I play guitar and sing in a hard rock trio called "Octane" in Brazil. You can find us on MySpace and YouTube. As far as my favorite groups go, I like Avenged Sevenfold, Story of the Year, and System of a Down. From the "Old School" I love Iron Maiden and Metallica. I also like pop and classical music. I love Beethoven, Bach, and Mozart. I don't understand classical music, but I appreciate it so much. I like some Brazilian pop music but I really dislike, (I don't want to say hate, it's a strong word)… SAMBA! Samba's the national music of Brazil. It's upbeat and encourages listeners to dance. It's not for me, though.

So all of you who may have questions for me, please post them on the Papercutz Blog and

I'll try to answer as quickly as possible! My favorite titles from THE HARDY BOYS so far are #8: "A Hardy Day's Night" (just a beautiful father and son story) and #15: "Live Free, Die Hardy!" which was action-packed. I've got to thank Jim Salicrup, Terry Nantier, Scott Lobdell, Laurie E. Smith, and Mark Lerer for all of their hard work and support. Perhaps most importantly, thanks to THE HARDY BOYS fans! Without you we wouldn't be able to put these great graphic novels together. Thanks and be sure to ask me questions!

–